THE MYSTERY OF THE
LOST WILL

THE MYSTERY OF THE LOST WILL

Jack Yerby

Cover Design by Sarah J. Yourzek
Illustrations by Hanna Al-Shaer

CRIMSON
DRAGON
PUBLISHING

Printed in the United States of America
First Edition 2021
ISBN 978-1-944644-09-3
Ebook 978-1-944644-14-7
Library of Congress Control Number: 2020946873

Young Adult/Mysteries & Detective Stories,
Action & Adventure, Survival

Crimson Dragon Publishing
Willow Alaska
www.crimsondragonpublishing.com

Contents

Also by Jack Yerby: *Mystery of the Haunted House: Chapter 1*

The Mystery of the Lost Will

Chapter 1
How To Change a Will

The war-torn boulevard was littered with wrecked and burning cars, the perfect place for an ambush. Kalani peered over the hood of the charred Hummer where he had taken cover. He didn't see any sign of the enemy hunting him.

He scanned the tops of the buildings looking for snipers. *It would be just like them to post someone up there when there are so many more places to hide down here at street level*, he thought. He didn't see anything suspicious, but a nagging feeling that something was wrong kept bothering him.

Turning to his brother sitting on the ground to his right leaning against the Hummer's rear tire, he whispered, "Tristen, cover me while I run to that wrecked Toyota on the curb over there on the left. I'm gonna get them in a crossfire."

Tristen nodded his head, got up, moved around his brother to the front of the Hummer, and sighted his rifle over its hood. Kalani moved right to the rear of the Hummer and stopped, careful to stay concealed behind the vehicle's protective bulk.

He scanned the empty doors and windows of the stores on the right side of the street. He didn't want a surprise attack from behind him when he darted for his new position.

He saw what remained of beautiful shops once filled with happy shoppers, their care-free excitement filling the storefronts with noise and bustle. But the war had changed all that, destroying the buildings, leaving them hulking, empty shells, silent, with gaping holes in their walls. Now, the only sound he heard was the crackling of a fire burning out of control behind him a block away.

The avenue where he and his brother were pinned down was wide, with four lanes for traffic and a fifth down the center for turning. The Hummer the two boys crouched behind sat crossways in the middle lane, its nose pointed to the left.

Kalani would have to move fast if he wanted to cross three open lanes to reach his new position safely. He planned to dash from the rear of the Hummer rather than the front even though that end was closer to his new cover. Just maybe the enemy rifles would be aimed at the wrong spot on the Hummer when he bolted from his cover.

Kalani took a deep breath and prepared for

his run. The acrid smell of the Hummer's burnt upholstery stung his nose.

With a final, deep breath, he ran for his new position. He zigzagged to make himself a harder target for the enemy who had him and his brother pinned down.

One lane. Good!

Two lanes. Very good!

Three lanes. I'm gonna make it!

BLAM! BLAM!

Kalani was hit, and he knew he wouldn't reach the Toyota as his vision blurred and turned gray. *I almost made it,* he thought as everything went black.

Kalani turned to his brother and whacked him on the shoulder. "I thought you were going to cover me," he said, his voice filled with frustration and disappointment.

"Hey, they got me too!" Tristen said rubbing his shoulder. Kalani may be tall and thin, but he still packed a wicked wallop when he got frustrated.

Kalani heard laughter in his headphones. "Gotcha both! The Rez Warrior strikes again!"

"You wouldn't have if my brother had covered me like he was supposed to," Kalani said. He hit the "off" button on the Play Station console. "Anyway, I'm tired of playing video games," he added into the mic attached to his headset. "Come on over, Danner, and I'll beat you in basketball."

Kalani heard his friend laugh again. "Not if we play Rez-ball, you won't."

"That's because there *aren't* any rules the way you guys play basketball on the Reservation!"

Danner laughed once more. "Okay, I'll be there in a little while. I gotta to take my grandma to Walmart."

Kalani groaned. His friend was full-blooded Navajo and operated on "Navajo time." Which meant he would arrive when he arrived. Sometimes his friend's lackadaisical sense of punctuality drove Kalani crazy, especially when he was bored and wanted to do something with his classmate.

"Let's go outside and shoot some hoops," Kalani said to his brother. "It's too nice a day to spend indoors."

∽

It was over an hour later when Danner finally arrived at the Henderson home in his beat-up old Ford pickup, the Rez Rocket as he called it.

"Boy, am I glad you showed up," Kalani said when his friend drove up and parked in the dirt road in front of his house. "Tristen isn't much competition for me."

"Whadya expect out of a wrestler?" his brother said, taking a shot at the basket. "I'm not a giraffe like you two." He arced the ball over Kalani's head while his older brother was distracted by the arrival of their tall, thin Navajo friend. Tristen's shot went wide, not even hitting the backboard.

"Here, let me show you how it's done," said Danner running to catch the ball before it went into the garage. He bounced it to get a feel for its firmness as he walked to the seam by the road at the far end of the concrete driveway that marked their half-court boundary. Kalani placed himself between his friend and the basket and spread his arms and legs in a good defensive posture as Danner started dribbling toward him. But rather than trying to go around Kalani, Danner lowered his shoulder and bumped him hard, knocking him to the ground.

"Hey, that was a foul!" Kalani said as he watched Danner's lay-up go through the basket with a swish.

"I didn't hear a ref's whistle," his friend said with a grin. He caught the ball under the basket and passed it to Kalani who, now back on his feet, caught it easily.

"Okay, Rez-ball it is," he said as he charged his classmate with a heavy bump of his own and made his lay-up.

"What took you so long getting here," Kalani asked as he passed his friend the ball and the two boys started their game of reservation style, rough-and-tumble basketball. Tristen sat down on the lawn in the cool shade of a Navajo Willow to watch their game of cutthroat one-on-one.

"I saw the DeVille twins test-driving a new Corvette at Walmart when I took Grandma there," Danner said, rushing past Kalani and making a basket. "They were showing off how rich they are by test driving a new sports car. Or how rich they will be as soon as they inherit old Wyatt Granger's fortune."

"Who's he?" said Kalani, catching the ball Danner had passed him after his shot.

"Wyatt was an eccentric old man with more money than good sense. Or at least, that's what my grandma tells me," said Danner as he spread his arms and legs, ready to block Kalani's drive. "He had a trading post on the Rez. But he didn't make much money from the store because a lot of time he let his customers pay for stuff with their turquoise jewelry when they didn't have any cash."

Kalani backed up to the half-court boundary to start his run at the basket, and Danner continued his explanation. "My grandma says old man Granger was too soft hearted for his own good and soon ended up with a ton of handmade jewelry and very little money. Sometimes his customers returned to buy their stuff back, but most of the time they didn't. Instead, they simply made more, then came in and traded it for more groceries. Over the years he collected a lot of jewelry but was always broke because he couldn't sell any of it. Back then, Indian jewelry wasn't worth much."

"Sounds like a good way to go bankrupt," said

Kalani as he juked around Danner and made his layup. "How did he get rich?" as he passed the ball to his classmate.

"When the internet was invented, he put his turquoise up for sale," said Danner. "That was about the same time Indian jewelry became fashionable in the big cities back east. He sold his jewelry for a whole lot more than the credit he gave his customers. Then once he saw how popular Indian stuff was, he began to buy more jewelry and even Navajo rugs to sell online."

"Why are the DeVille twins inheriting his money?" asked Kalani. "Are they related to Wyatt?"

"Yeah, Wyatt was the uncle of Melvin DeVille, their dad."

Danner dribbled toward the basket and continued his explanation. "He was living with the DeVille family when he suddenly up and died last winter. My grandma told me that just as he was dying, he tried to say something to the nurse in his hospital room. But he was too weak to get out what he wanted to tell her."

"How does your grandma know that?" Kalani asked.

"From my aunt. She's a nurse's aide, and Melvin hired her to take care of Wyatt while he lived with 'em. She was at the hospital standing at the foot of his bed to switch his shoes as soon as he died. She saw Wyatt try to whisper something to the nurse, but he couldn't get it out before he passed."

"Switch his shoes?" said Kalani. "Switch them for what?"

"No," answered Danner, "she wasn't switching them for another pair of shoes or anything like that. Wyatt was in bed and barefoot. My aunt was going to put his shoes on him after he died but reversed—the left shoe on the right foot and the right shoe on the left foot."

"Why was she going to do that?" asked Kalani, puzzled, standing up out of his defensive posture. "Why not leave him barefoot?"

"It's an old Navajo custom," said Danner taking advantage of Kalani's inattention to drive for the basket. He made an easy shot.

"It's believed the ghost of a dead person returns to where it lived if it has an unfinished task to do. The shoes are reversed on the feet of the body to keep the spirit from following its tracks back home. The tracks will be backwards and confuse it."

"But why switch the shoes of Wyatt Granger?" said Kalani, catching the ball Danner had passed to him. "That's a *Dineh* custom, and he was a *bilagana*."

"Oh, I'm impressed!" said Danner "You used the words for *Navajo* and *non-Navajo* correctly. Pretty good for a *bilagana* new-comer to New Mexico."

Danner got ready to block Kalani as he continued his story.

"My aunt wanted to honor old man Granger when he died. He was really kind and understanding to us *Dineh*. He let us buy stuff with our turquoise and sometimes let us buy more than what it was worth. He also observed a lot of *Dineh* customs and even learned to speak Navajo. It was right to honor him when he died."

"So then, he got rich when Navajo jewelry and rugs became hot stuff, huh?" said Kalani, not moving but bouncing the ball at the end of the driveway.

"Yeah, and that's when Melvin started to take an interest in him."

Kalani stopped bouncing the ball and tucked it under one arm. "What do you mean? What happened?"

"Before Old Man Granger began to sell stuff on the internet, he was poor, I mean *really* poor, so poor he had to live with relatives. But they were as broke as he was and couldn't afford him living with them for very long. So, the old man constantly moved from one family member to another. I heard that when he was broke, Melvin had nothing to do with him. But once he got rich, Melvin got friendly and convinced him to move in with his family. Wyatt lived with the DeVilles for about a year before he died around Christmas. I guess he left his entire fortune to Melvin from what Akron and Tulsa said today at Walmart."

"Is that the name of the DeVille twins?" asked

Tristen from under the tree. "They're named after two cities back east?"

Danner nodded with a smile on his face. "Yeah, they are. But it could be worse. They could be named Dallas and Denver."

All three of the boys started laughing at this idea.

5

After supper that evening, Kalani watched as Tristen worked out in their basement home gym.

Kalani was tall and lanky, blond, sixteen years old, and about to enter his junior year in high school. Earlier that spring in the middle of the high school basketball season, he and his family had moved from Houston to Flora Vista, a little town in northwest New Mexico. As a result, Kalani had missed playing his favorite sport at his new school. But in pick-up games with some of the varsity players, he knew for certain he would make the high school's team next year.

Tristen was two years younger and obviously his half-brother. Short and stocky with dark hair, his favorite sports were football and wrestling. Since he would be entering his freshman year when school started, he planned to go out for both teams and wanted to be in shape for try-outs.

But Kalani soon got bored watching Tristen lift weights and went upstairs. He wanted to get back on his Play Station with his Navajo friend, but his dad had strict rules about no video games at night. Mason Henderson believed that evenings were family time.

Kalani walked into the den and plopped down on a long couch facing the fireplace. The couch was placed in the large, main room of the Henderson house in such a way as to divide it into two areas: the dining room and the family room. His dad was sitting in the family room portion in a big, overstuffed easy chair checking email on his laptop.

After a few moments of silence, his dad looked up from his computer. "You seem awfully quiet tonight. What's on your mind?"

Kalani looked over at his dad who always seemed to read him like an open book. It was part of what made them so close.

"Pop, what do you have to do to change your will?" Kalani asked.

Mason looked at his son over the top of his reading glasses, his voice serious but his eyes playful, "Do you have a will made out already, one you plan to change?"

"No, I was thinking of old Mr. Granger."

"What about him?" asked his father, closing his laptop. Kalani was glad he had a father who took an active interest in him. He had friends back in Houston whose parents didn't seem to care about their children, never taking the time to sit and talk with them about what was important in their lives. They always seemed lonely. And envious of Kalani.

"He made a huge fortune selling Navajo jewelry on the internet," Kalani said. "It would be a shame if that awful DeVille family got it all."

"Why do you say the DeVilles are so awful," asked his dad, a little surprised at his son.

"I've seen the twins at school and watched how they act when there are no teachers around. They pick on the little freshmen and make fun of Navajo kids with their accents. They're so arrogant with their noses up in the air—I'm surprised they don't drown when it rains."

"That's because they live here in the desert, and it doesn't rain much," said his dad with a grin. "Now, if they lived in Houston, they might be in some serious danger."

Kalani laughed and enjoyed the moment of shared humor with his father.

"Right now, Mr. DeVille stands to inherit all of Wyatt Granger's huge fortune. And if he does, his twins will be even more unbearable when school starts next fall."

"If they're anything like their dad, I'd have to agree with you," said his dad. "Melvin isn't the most likeable person I've ever met. He seems to think he's above the law. I've pulled him over a couple of times for not having his seat belt on. I never wrote him a ticket. Instead, I only gave him a warning. But every time I've stopped him, he was just on the verge of being disrespectful."

Kalani knew that even though his dad worked for the county sheriff's department as a criminal investigator, he could still issue traffic tickets. And Kalani planned to obey every last law on the books once he got his driver's license. His dad might be willing to cut Melvin some slack from time to time, but he knew that same generosity would not be extended to him.

"What makes you think Wyatt Granger was going to change his will?" Mason asked. "Did you have a serious, man-to-man talk with him before he died?" His dad grinned at his son's seriousness.

"No," replied Kalani, "all I know is what Danner told me today—how he moved from one family member to another before he got rich. But I was thinking that if he was so kind to his Navajo customers, it seems that he would have left something in his will to those relatives who took him in from time to time."

Mason silently nodded his head in agreement.

"Danner also said his aunt was there when he died," Kalani continued. "He attempted to whisper something to the nurse in her ear but didn't have the strength to finish what he was trying to say."

Again, his dad nodded.

"It's been bugging me all day, ever since Danner told me about him. I wonder if Mr. Granger did change his will and was trying to tell the nurse about it."

"It's strange you should come up with that idea," said his dad. "A little bit before he died, I overheard Wyatt talking with Damon Weems about wills in the county courthouse."

"Who's he?" asked Kalani.

"He's a lawyer who specializes in wills and probate," his dad answered. "I heard them discussing what it would take to make a will legal, and if a lawyer would be necessary. I've often wondered myself if Wyatt ever wrote a second will."

He paused for a moment, thinking, before he continued.

"I know Damon pretty well from a class on New Mexico law I took before I moved you boys and your mother here from Houston. I had to pass it before I could start my job with the sheriff's department. Damon taught it, and I enrolled after it had already started. He tutored me on the side to get me caught up, and we've been good friends ever since. I think I'll ask him to lunch to see if Wyatt ever wrote another will."

About that time, Tristen came up from the basement covered in sweat, his workout finished. A big grin spread over his face when he saw his brother sitting on the couch with his back to him. Tiptoeing up behind Kalani, Tristen bent over the back and hugged his older brother around the neck.

"Yuck, get off me, you stinky pig!" said Kalani. "You're hot and sweaty!"

"Stinky pig, huh?" Tristen said. "Just for that, it's rassling time."

And with that, Tristen reached under Kalani's arms and yanked him up and over the back of the couch. As he slammed his tall, skinny brother down to the floor, he wrapped his short, muscular legs around him and moved his arms into position to put his brother in a painful wrestling move called the guillotine. It was Tristen's favorite move, and his opponents often pinned themselves in order to make the pain stop. Kalani wasn't going to be so lucky.

"You boys don't tear anything up," their father said, opening up his laptop and pushing his reading glasses back up the bridge of his nose. "If you do, be sure to clean it up before your mother gets back. She'll be home soon from her meeting."

They only broke one lamp.

Chapter 2
Replacing a Lamp

Early the next morning, Kalani awoke to knocking on his bedroom door. Fearing it might be his younger brother with another wrestling match in mind, he got up, braced his knee against the door, and carefully cracked it open. He peered through the narrow gap.

"Oh, it's you, Pop," he said as he moved back and opened the door wide. "I thought it was Tristen."

"You boys owe your mother a new lamp," said Mason Henderson as he entered the room. "She pretended not to notice the one in the den was missing, but she asked about it after you two went to bed."

"It's all Tristen's fault!" Kalani said defensively. "He started it."

"That may be true," said his dad as he reached into his hip pocket for his wallet. "But I want you two to go to the mall in Farmington and buy her another lamp." He handed his son a credit card. "Buy one just like the one you broke. And nothing else—no video games."

He put the wallet back in his hip pocket. "I'm trying to arrange lunch with Damon Weems today to ask if Wyatt Granger ever made out a second will. You want to join us?"

"Sure, Pop," Kalani said eagerly. "Where do you want to meet?"

"Dad's Diner is right by the mall. Why don't we eat there. I'll text you what time to meet us."

As he left the room, he turned back to his son and said, "Remember, just a lamp with my credit card. Nothing else!"

He turned away and left the room with a grin on his face.

ᔕ

"Dude, how many more stores are you going to check out?" asked Tristen. "You've hit every single one in the mall already. Twice!"

"Oh, stop it," said Kalani. "There is only one more we haven't been to yet. If we don't find anything better in here, we'll go back to Penny's and get the lamp we saw there."

"I don't know why we didn't get it in the first place," said Tristen. "We both thought Mom would like it. And it wasn't expensive. Right now, we could be playing video games in the Fun Factory. But no-ooh, you've got to hit every shop in the mall selling lamps to see if they've got a better one than what we saw in Penny's."

"Stop whining," said Kalani as he led his brother into the mall's last unvisited shop. "We wouldn't be shopping for a lamp if you hadn't put me in that guillotine last night."

"No, we wouldn't be shopping for a lamp if your legs weren't eighteen feet long and you hadn't been flopping around like a dying fish," said Tristen. "You're the one who kicked the table and knocked over the lamp."

"That guillotine hurt!"

"It was meant to. You were supposed to tap out when I put you in it."

"You wouldn't have let me up if I had tapped out."

"Yes, I would," said Tristen.

Then he grinned. "Eventually."

Kalani gave his brother a dirty look.

After a quick look in the household goods section of the store, Kalani said to his brother, "Okay, let's go back to Penny's. I like the one we found there better."

"Finally!" said Tristen. "You drive me nuts sometimes being so O C D about everything. You

The Mystery of the Lost Will

should just go with the flow like me—do things on the spur of the moment. You over-plan everything."

Kalani held the door open for his brother. "Yeah, but when you 'go with the flow,' you sometimes get swept away down the drain. And into the sewer!"

He led his brother down the inside courtyard of the mall towards Penny's. "Remember that race last year when you crashed your BMX bike into a tree covered with poison ivy because you had a 'spur of the moment' impulse to take a shortcut? There was a good reason they didn't want racers going through those trees."

They arrived at Penny's and Kalani again held the door open for his brother. "You itched for a week. Mom had to put boxing gloves on you to keep you from scratching all those welts and spreading the rash. I laughed my butt off."

This time Tristen gave the dirty look.

Inside, they headed toward the rear of the store where they had seen the lamp they planned to buy. But before they had taken a dozen steps, Kalani grabbed Tristen on his shoulder. "Oh, don't look now, but there's Akron and Tulsa DeVille over there by that display table."

The boys stopped and watched as a teenage boy and girl Kalani's age pawed through a pile of jeans on a large table. They watched as the two held up pair after pair, looked at them in disgust, then threw them back down, unfolded, in a crumpled heap. A couple of them landed on the floor.

Kalani saw another teenage girl wearing a Penny's name tag come out from where the dressing rooms were located. He recognized her from school and was about to go over to say hi. But he changed his mind when he saw her approach the twins and ask if she could help them find something. He didn't want to interrupt her while she was assisting customers.

"Don't you have anything that isn't so ugly?" Kalani heard Tulsa ask. "I've seen better looking clothes at a garage sale!" She dropped the jeans she had been holding on the floor, a grimace on her face.

The salesclerk picked them up and folded them neatly.

"These are the latest look from Levi's. All the kids will be wearing them at school next year."

"Maybe the trailer trash living up on Crouch Mesa. Or the Navajos with no money out on the Rez," said Tulsa with an arrogant tone of voice. "These are about the only clothes THOSE kinds of people can afford."

"Hmph, not us," said Akron. "When we get our inheritance, we'll be shopping at Macy's in Albuquerque. Or maybe we'll just jet over to Neiman Marcus in Dallas for our school clothes."

Kalani backed away from the embarrassing scene and herded Tristen toward the household goods area of the store.

"I see what you mean about them being scum-bags," said Tristen once they were out of ear shot of the arrogant twins. "They're still giving that salesgirl grief over the jeans," as he peered back over his shoulder.

"I feel sorry for her being picked on like that," said Kalani. "I've seen her around school, and she seems pretty cool. She certainly doesn't deserve to be treated like that."

Kalani searched the shelves for a few minutes and found a boxed-up lamp. Tucking it under his arm, he led Tristen to the cashier's station, but there was no one at the register. He looked around and saw the salesgirl from school heading towards him. On the display table behind her were all the jeans, now neatly folded. It looked like the DeVille twins had never touched them. The arrogant siblings were not in sight; Kalani figured they had left the store.

She arrived at the checkout counter, and Kalani handed her the boxed lamp and his father's credit card. As she scanned the lamp's bar code and ran the card through the card reader, he smiled at her. "You got those jeans folded back up pretty fast. You have to do that often?"

"Not the whole stack," she answered, as she waited for the sales transaction to go through. "I can't believe those jerks unfolded every single pair on that table, even the ones that obviously wouldn't fit them."

The transaction came back approved, and she tore off the ticket and handed it to Kalani.

"I shouldn't have called them jerks," she apologized as Kalani signed the receipt and handed it back to her. "But they really got on my nerves. I live up on Crouch Mesa, and we're not trailer trash."

"Yeah, my best friend is Navajo and lives out on the Reservation," he replied. "I got kinda mad at them for implying that all the *Dineh* living on the Rez were poor."

She nodded her head in agreement as she put the boxed lamp in a bag and handed Kalani his receipt. "I don't know why they're being so arrogant with that attitude. They're not rich themselves."

"They're supposed to inherit a huge fortune from a guy named Wyatt Granger," he explained.

"Not from what they were saying just a few minutes ago," she said. "I overheard them talking while I was refolding the jeans. They said that they won't get the money until the lawyers stop bickering."

"What would the lawyers be arguing about?"

"The girl said the old man's will has been tied up in probate court so long their father thinks someone is looking for a second will or something. She said they may not get any money until after school starts. They may even have to come back here to buy their school clothes."

"It would serve them right if they didn't get any inheritance at all," said Kalani.

"Yeah, I agree. And I'd love to be the clerk who gets to cash them out when they gotta come back here for their clothes."

Kalani grinned at his classmate. He thought such a come-uppance would be perfect. He hoped he could witness it.

∽

Mason Henderson felt someone grab his shoulders and squeeze them as he sat looking at a menu at a table in Dad's Diner. Turning around, he saw his eldest son grinning down at him from his six-foot three-inch height.

"Was that supposed to hurt?" he asked. "If so, you need to get your brother to show you how to lift weights."

Turning to a distinguished looking man in his early fifties sitting across from him, he said, "Damon, I'd like you to meet my two boys, Kalani and Tristen."

"Very pleased to meet you," Kalani said formally as he shook his dad's guest's hand. Tristen was mute when he shook hands. His freshman shyness had kicked in.

"I understand you boys were out shopping for new lamps," said Damon with a grin as the Henderson brothers sat down. "I've got two boys of my own, so

I know that sometimes wrestling matches can get a little out of hand."

Kalani blushed as he glanced over at his father. He was embarrassed that his dad had told his lawyer friend about the wrestling accident. Mason chuckled at seeing his eldest son become flustered and lose some of his brash self-confidence.

"Where's the lamp?" he asked as Kalani picked up a menu and looked it over.

"I put it in the back seat of your battle wagon," he answered. "We parked our bikes right next to it."

Damon looked over at Mason, his eyebrows raised in a silent question.

"They call my police SUV a 'battle wagon' because my riot gear, weapons and ammunition are stored in it," said Mason. "They ride Honda Rebel 250 motorcycles."

Turning to Kalani he held his hand out and cleared his throat, "uh-hum."

"Oh yeah, I almost forgot," said Kalani as he handed his dad the credit card and receipt. "You'll be glad to know that we didn't buy anything else with it. Even though Tristen was looking at another game for our Play Station."

"Hey, that's not fair!" exclaimed Tristen. "YOU were the one who said we should stop by the store to look at video games! I was only browsing. We left because I was starving and didn't want to wait for you to decide which one you wanted."

Kalani glared at his brother, then grinned sheepishly at his father.

"Now I understand how the lamp got broken," said Damon, with a laugh.

5

"Mr. Weems, does a lawyer have to write a will for it to be legal?" Kalani asked as the waitress cleared their table of some of the plates after lunch.

"You planning on getting one?" he responded with a grin. "Are you about to die and want to make sure your fortune goes to someone in particular?"

Kalani looked surprise. "No, I was just wondering what it would take to rewrite a will, to change who was included in it."

"Don't worry; your father loves you very much and isn't planning on dropping you from his will."

Kalani gave another start and quickly added, "No, not my dad. Wyatt Granger."

Kalani saw the lawyer glace at his dad, the grin replaced by a question on his face.

"He's thinking that Wyatt may have written another will," Mason explained. "I told him about overhearing you and Wyatt discussing wills last winter in the courthouse."

Damon Weems paused as if thinking before he

continued in a more serious voice. "Yes, we did discuss what it would take to make a will legal."

"What did you tell him?" Kalani asked.

"That it had to be validated by a notary public."

"What's a rotary public," asked Tristen, looking up from the salad he was still eating.

"Not 'rotary' but 'notary,'" explained his father. "It's like a legal witness, someone who verifies that your signature is really yours, and that no one else is signing your name to a document. If they don't know you personally, you have to have positive proof that you are who you say you are."

"That way, no one could claim to be Wyatt Granger and write a fake will," said Kalani.

"Exactly," said his dad.

"Why the interest in Wyatt Granger?" asked Damon.

"My best friend told me his aunt was there at Wyatt's deathbed, and she saw him trying to say something to the nurse attending him," explained Kalani. "But he never got whatever was on his mind out to her."

"And you think he was talking about another will?" asked Damon.

"Well, I hope so," Kalani went on. "Those DeVille twins are arrogant enough without inheriting Mr. Granger's fortune."

"Well," said Damon hesitating a moment, "you know I'm not supposed to discuss a client's business without their permission. Lawyer-client confidentiality and all that."

"Yeah, but your client is dead, so he can't be asked for permission. And, it's not going to hurt him or his reputation in any way."

"True, and we didn't discuss a new will in the privacy of my office," Damon said to Kalani. Looking over at his dad, he continued, "As I recall, Wyatt and I were standing in the hall waiting for the elevator. You were right behind us and got on with us. So that makes what I told him in the elevator public knowledge."

"I believe you also instructed him to let you see it before he had it notarized," added Mason.

"Yes, I did. But he never brought me a second will to look over."

Damon paused and thought for a moment. "I remember the following day I closed my office for a couple of weeks. It was Christmas break, and I took my boys to Telluride for a family ski vacation since they both had several weeks off from college. When I got back into town, I read in the paper that Wyatt had died."

"Do you think he ever wrote a second will?" asked Kalani in the pause that followed.

"He could have, but there's no way to be sure. All I know is that he was very interested in knowing how to change one."

"I'll bet he did change it," said Kalani. "All we

have to do is find the notary who witnessed his signature."

"Good luck with that!" said Damon. "Do you know how many there are in San Juan county?"

Kalani shook his head slowly.

"Hundreds!" said Damon. And he chuckled at Kalani's surprised expression.

Chapter 3
Marbles and Raindrops

Early the next morning, Kalani poked his head
into his brother's bedroom. "Hey, get up. Pop wants us
downstairs."

Tristen mumbled something incoherent and
rolled over on his side, away from the door.

"Okay, you asked for it," Kalani said under his
breath as he tiptoed into the room. He grinned as
he looked down at what he held in his hand: a large,
pewter mug filled with marbles. He guessed there
were over a hundred of them. Their mother kept
them in the freezer which meant they were ice cold.
This was her standard way of getting her sons up
for school when they were slow to get out of bed. It
worked better than a glass of water because it didn't
get the sheets wet.

Kalani quickly lifted the covers off his brother
and poured the marbles along his back and legs into
the trough his body created where he pushed down

the mattress. Tristen shrieked and rolled away from the icy marbles. But try as he would, he wasn't able to out-roll them. He shrieked again and leaped out of bed.

"Okay! Okay! I'm up!" he snapped as he shivered. He could still feel the freezing cold along his back and legs.

"Come on. Pop's got a chore for us today," said Kalani, handing the now empty mug to his brother. "And don't forget to put the marbles back."

That was part of the punishment for taking too long to get out of bed when called. The late sleeper had to get all the marbles from the bed and put them back in the mug.

Down in the breakfast nook by the kitchen, Kalani finished his stack of pancakes as Tristen came stumbling down the stairs. Kalani shook his head sadly; his brother was definitely not a morning person.

"I saved you some pancakes," Kalani said as he got up to rinse off his plate and put it in the dishwasher.

"Only because I *told* him to save you some," said Tamala Henderson, not looking up from her laptop. She was seated beside her husband at the breakfast table.

Mason looked up at his youngest son from a small stack of papers in front of him. "I was going to give you two more minutes to get downstairs before releasing the Kraken on your share," as he nodded toward Tristen's older brother. Kalani was always hungry, and his parents were constantly amazed at how much he could eat.

Tristen scowled at his brother as he put the mug of marbles back in the freezer.

After Tristen got his pancakes from the kitchen counter and sat down at the table, Mason Henderson put his papers in a large brown envelope and looked at his sons. "I want you two to ride into Aztec and take these papers to the county clerk's office. They have to be entered in the records today, and I've got to drive down to Albuquerque in just a few minutes. Aztec is in the other direction, and I don't have time to run them to the courthouse before I get on the road."

"Can we take the pickup?" asked Kalani, trying to keep the excitement out of his voice.

"Nice try," his father answered. "And just who is going to be the adult in the vehicle with you?"

He handed his empty coffee cup to his eldest son and nodded toward the dishwasher. "You only have your temporary license, so there has to be an adult with you in the front seat when you drive."

Kalani took his dad's cup to the sink, rinsed it, and put it in the dishwasher. "But the pickup would be faster than our bikes. And safer on the highway, too."

"Sorry, but no dice," his father replied. "And since when are you worried about riding your Hondas on the highway? Your 250's are street legal, and you certainly didn't mind riding them into Farmington yesterday for lunch." He grinned at his eldest son. "Don't worry; you'll get your regular license as soon as you finish fifty hours of driving time with an adult."

As Kalani sat back down at the table, his dad handed him the thick envelop. "Take these to the county clerk's office, have them recorded, and bring me back the receipt."

"Yes sir," Kalani answered. "Do you mind if I check with someone there and get a list of all the notaries in the area? Or do Tristen and I need to be back home right away?"

"You still think there's another will out there?" his mother asked with a chuckle. "You're like a bulldog. Once you get something in your teeth, you don't let go."

After exchanging a glance with his wife, Mason said, "Go ahead and take a look at the county records if you want, but don't be a pest doing it. Don't get in the way of the workers in the office. Your mother gets off work at five, and I won't be back from Albuquerque until late tonight. Just make sure you two are home in time to help her with supper."

∽

"Wow! Look at all those names!" exclaimed Tristen, peering over his brother's shoulder. "You wouldn't think there would be so many rotaries in the county."

"Notaries," his brother corrected.

Kalani was seated at a computer in the county courthouse as his brother stood behind him. On the screen was a list of everyone in San Juan County licensed to be a notary public. After registering the papers for their dad, Kalani had asked if he could get a list of notaries in the area. The lady behind the counter had taken the boys over to a public computer in the room and had shown Kalani how to log on and get the information he had asked for.

"There's no way we can ask each one if they witnessed Wyatt Granger's signature on a will," said Tristen.

"Yeah, but we can check the ones located in Farmington. That's where he was living with the DeVilles when he died."

"Are we going to go visit each person one at a time and ask them about Wyatt? That will take forever."

"Hmm, maybe we can just call them. There's a phone number by each name."

Kalani moved the mouse over the drop-down menus on the screen looking for a way to print the information he wanted. He scrolled around for a few seconds, clicked the mouse, and looked around for the printer. He heard it printing behind the counter and walked over to the sound. The clerk who had helped him with the computer picked up the printout, counted the pages, and brought them over to the counter where Kalani was standing.

"Is there a fee for printing that out?" Kalani asked the lady.

"You're Mason Henderson's son, right?"

"Yes, ma'am," he answered.

"No charge," she responded. "Your dad's a nice guy. He always says *ma'am* to me even though he's older than I am."

"That's his Texas upbringing. He thumps me on the head if I forget to say *ma'am* or *sir* to adults."

"Good for him," she replied. "It's nice to see polite kids."

$$\backsim$$

In the parking lot of the county courthouse many minutes later, Tristen said to his older brother. "Let's go back home on the Old Aztec Highway."

"Why?" Kalani asked. "It will take longer. It winds a lot and we'll have to go a lot slower than on the main highway."

"True, but there are lots of trees lining it, and it's narrow enough we'll be in the shade most of the time. It's too hot to drive on the highway."

"I don't know. We might get caught in that storm heading this way," Kalani said. He looked over at the horizon and saw big thunderheads building in the distance.

"Naw, I think we'll make it home before the storm hits," Tristen answered as he glanced up at the sky. "Those clouds are way off. It's still clear overhead."

ᔕ

As the boys rode down the old road that connected Aztec and Flora Vista, Kalani kept glancing up at the sky. "We'd better pick up the pace if we want to get home before this storm hits."

But as he said it, he realized that he couldn't hear his brother's motorcycle behind him. He snuck a quick glance over his shoulder and saw Tristen off his bike, walking it. Kalani turned around in the narrow road and rode back to him.

"What's up?" he asked Tristen.

"I ran out of gas," his brother answered.

"You didn't bother to check your gas gauge before we left Aztec?!"

"Hey, I've ridden on *Empty* longer than this before!"

Kalani began to weave from one side of the road to the other in order to keep his balance as Tristen walked his bike down the road.

"Oh man, this storm is going to catch us for

sure, and we're going to get soaked," said Kalani as he looked up at the sky.

"Don't worry about it," said Tristen. "You've got nothing to sweat. Horse turds don't melt. They even float." And he laughed.

Kalani glared at him, then got off his bike to walk alongside his brother.

A few minutes later Kalani felt the first fat raindrops splash on his helmet. "I *told* you that we'd get caught in this storm. Now, we're gonna get drenched."

"This way," shouted Tristen as he suddenly turned left down a narrow lane leading away from the road.

He led his brother about a hundred yards to where the lane ended in front of an old house and a dilapidated barn. The barn door was open, and Tristen led his brother inside just as a loud crash of thunder sounded and the rain started pouring down.

"Hope the owner doesn't mind us riding out this storm in his barn," Kalani said to Tristen as the two boys lowered the kickstands of their bikes and walked over to the entrance to watch the downpour.

"He doesn't," came a voice from the shadows of the barn behind them.

Chapter 4
The Gas Can Clue

Kalani turned to see who had spoken and saw a teenage boy about his own age walking toward him. He was wiping his greasy hands on a dirty, red, garage rag and smelled faintly of oily engine parts.

"Thanks for letting us wait out of the storm in here," Kalani said. "We thought we could make it back to Flora Vista before it started raining, but we didn't."

"No problem," said the boy. "These summer thunderstorms build up quick then disappear just as fast. You're both welcome to stay in here until the rain stops."

"I'm Kalani Henderson by the way, and this is my brother, Tristen," said Kalani extending his hand.

"Dillon Gunderson," replied the teen. He wiped his hand once more before shaking Kalani's. "Excuse the grease. I was working on an engine when I heard you come in."

"You're a mechanic?" asked Kalani.

"Yeah, kinda," replied Dillon. "More of a shade tree mechanic."

"Then why are you in a barn and not under a tree?" asked Tristen.

"That means he's not school-trained," explained Kalani. "He just has a natural talent for working on engines and stuff."

Dillon looked down at his feet and said quietly, "Yeah, I'm kinda self-taught. But I do want to go to school and learn to work on small engines. That way, my brother and I could open our own shop and work on all kinds of motorcycles."

"Where would you want to open your shop?" asked Kalani.

"Right here in this old barn," replied Dillon. "We already do some work here, but we don't have enough tools to do really complicated repairs. Or the money to buy more stuff."

Kalani looked into the shadowy interior and saw the parts of a motorcycle lying on a workbench and a few tools scattered about, lit by a flashlight that was still on. He guessed there was no electricity in the barn.

"Cool bikes, by the way," said Dillon nodding toward Kalani and Tristen's two motorcycles. "I saw you pushing them. What's wrong with 'em?"

"Ran out of gas," answered Tristen softly.

"I've got some here," said Dillon.

Kalani watched him walk over to his work

area and pick up a small gas can from under the workbench. It was so old that it was made of metal, not plastic like the one his dad kept in the bed of his pickup. And its once bright red color was faded to a brownish red, the color of dried blood.

Dillon walked over to the pair of bikes standing on their kickstands. "Which one needs gas?"

"That one," said Tristen, pointing to his bike.

As Dillon poured gas into the tank, Kalani gave a start. Printed in faded lettering on the side of the can were the words *W. Granger*.

∽

"Did that gas can once belong to Wyatt Granger?" asked Kalani as Dillon finished putting gas in Tristen's bike.

"Yeah, he used to live next door," answered Dillon as he screwed the cap back on the gas can. "Why? Did you know him?"

"No," replied Kalani. "But we've heard a lot about him lately. Seems like he was a really neat guy."

"Yeah, he was," Dillon said. "He used to help me and my brother out when we ran outta money."

Kalani looked at him, a silent question on his face.

"He would hire us to do odd jobs around his house next door."

Tristen looked at Kalani and said, "I thought he lived with relatives?"

"He did when he was broke," said Dillon, "But once he got rich, he bought the property next door."

"Then why did he go live with the DeVilles?" asked Tristen before Kalani could voice the same question.

"His nephew, Melvin, convinced him that it would be better to move in with him and his family," Dillon answered. "In case something happened to him."

"Like what?" asked Tristen.

"Oh, you know, in case he fell and couldn't get up. Or if he got sick, like he did that first winter he lived next door to us."

"What happened to him?" asked Kalani.

"He caught a really bad flu that was going around," answered Dillon. "Josh and I took care of him while he was sick. We took turns spending the night with him to make sure he kept warm and got something to eat."

"That sure was nice of you," said Tristen.

"Well, it's what anyone would do," replied Dillon. He looked shyly down at his feet.

Kalani didn't know what to say to ease Dillon's obvious embarrassment, so he changed the subject.

"How big is your shop here," he asked as he pointed toward the workbench area in the back of the barn.

"Not very big," Dillon said. He kept his eyes downcast on a pebble in the dirt and played with it with his foot. "Josh and I want to get more tools so we can handle bigger jobs. Right now, we're pretty limited in what we can do."

"Who's Josh, your father?" asked Tristen.

"My brother. Our parents died years ago, and Josh quit school to take care of me. He's out looking for more work for us right now."

"Is he a good mechanic like you?" asked Kalani.

Dillon's face brightened as he looked up from the pebble. "He's the best! He taught me everything I know about motorcycles. That's why I want to earn enough money to send him to San Juan College and their mechanical arts school. He'll learn a lot more, and then he'll teach me."

Kalani nodded his head in agreement. "Sounds like a good plan."

"Uncle Wyatt was going to leave us enough money to send one of us to school," Dillon said. "But when he died, we weren't mentioned in his will at all. At least, that's what Akron DeVille told us. He said his dad was going to get it all."

"Wyatt was your uncle?" asked Kalani.

"No, he wasn't really related to us; we just called him that," replied Dillon. "After the first winter when he caught that terrible flu, we became real good friends. I guess he noticed how we were struggling to get by on Josh's odd jobs. He used to have us do work at his place and then he would pay us more than it was worth. I remember one time he gave us each a hundred dollars just to rake up a pile of leaves and burn them. It took us less than an hour."

He paused and smiled as if recalling something fondly in his mind. "Sometimes there would be a bag of groceries on the front porch when I came home from school and Josh was out looking for work. I'm sure it was Uncle Wyatt who left them for us. He always seemed to know when we were out of food."

"I guess he was repaying you for taking care of him when he had the flu," said Tristen.

"No, it was more than that," answered Dillon. "Uncle Wyatt was just a really good guy, very kindhearted. That's why we started calling him Uncle. That seemed to please him a lot. He didn't have any kids of his own. We were probably the closest thing he had to family."

"What about his other relatives," asked Tristen. "You know, the ones who took him in when he didn't have any money."

"I know he had a niece and a nephew who took turns taking him in before he made his fortune," said Dillon. "I don't know how close he was to them. But I know neither one of them had much money to support him, so they could only keep him for a little while at a time. His nephew, Riley, works in the oil field on a drilling rig. But his job isn't steady. When he wasn't working, the money dried up. That's when

Uncle Wyatt would move in with his niece Kaylee and her husband, Kilian. He's a volunteer fireman in Aztec. Kaylee and Kilian were always broke because volunteers don't get paid and they lived on Kaylee's part-time job."

"You said that Wyatt was going to leave you and your brother enough money to send one of you to school?" asked Kalani. "When did he tell you that?"

"A couple of days before Christmas," answered Dillon. "He brought over a large turkey and a bunch of groceries. He said it was for our Christmas dinner."

"And you heard him say he was leaving you some money?"

"Yeah, but we didn't get to talk about it. Melvin, his nephew, got in a big hurry to leave. He was driving Uncle Wyatt around that day. When Uncle Wyatt started talking about his will, Mr. DeVille got really antsy and rushed him out of the house. He said they had lots of other places to go before dark. But I think he didn't want to hear about us being included in the will."

"I wonder if he also meant to include his nephew Riley and his niece Kaylee," said Kalani, more to himself.

"I don't know," said Dillon. "But you could ask them. They both live in Aztec."

About that time the sun broke through the clouds and the rain stopped. Kalani turned to his brother and said, "We'd better get on our way. It's getting pretty close to five o'clock, and Pop said to be home before Mom got off work."

Turning to Dillon, Kalani asked, "How much do we owe you for the gas?"

"Oh nothing," Dillon replied quickly. "Those 250's only hold about a gallon. I hardly put anything in your brother's cycle."

"Well, maybe we can repay you somehow one of these days."

Chapter 5
A Conference with Hamburgers

"Don't put the ice in the glasses yet. Mom's not home, and it will be melted by the time she fixes dinner," said Kalani sternly. "And the salad fork goes on the left, outside of the dinner fork." He reached over and moved the fork his brother had just set down to the other side of the plate.

"But I'm right-handed, so it should go on the right side of the plate," Tristen said. He moved the fork back to where he had first placed it.

"No, put it back where it belongs," said Kalani. He slapped the back of his brother's hand.

"Who says it belongs on the left?"

"Emily Post. And Mom."

Reluctantly Tristen moved the fork to the left of the dinner plate. "That's okay. I don't like salad anyway. I just won't eat any tonight, so it doesn't matter where I put that stupid fork."

Kalani scowled at his younger brother. "Yes, it does. Mom wants us to learn our table manners."

"How else are you going to learn to use good manners if you don't practice them at home?" Kalani added in a high-pitched, feminine voice.

Tristen laughed. "You sounded just like Mom when you said that."

"I do *not* sound like that!" said a voice behind them. Both boys jumped at the sudden noise.

"Sorry, Mom," Kalani said, his voice cowed. "Didn't know you were standing there. But Tristen wasn't setting the table right."

Tamala Henderson walked over to her sons and looked at the place settings. "They're correct."

"Yeah, after I made Tristen put his fork in the right place," said Kalani with a smug voice.

"What difference does it make where the dumb salad fork goes, anyway?" said Tristen. "Or why we have to have a separate fork for the salad?"

"When you're grown up and living on your own, you can eat any way you want. You can stuff your food into your mouth with a snow shovel for all I care," said their mother, "but while you're in my house, you'll use proper table manners. I don't want people to think you're being raised by wolves."

"Is that why you make us wear a shirt at the dinner table?" asked Tristen.

"Yes. And to take off your hat when you eat too," she added. "Both of those are considered very rude in many circles, and I don't want you two making fools of yourselves because you don't know any better."

"You boys listen to your mother," said their father as he came into the dining room from the kitchen. Again, both boys jumped at the sudden noise. He walked over to his wife, gave her a quick kiss, then took off his gun belt and set it down on the kitchen counter. "What's for supper?"

"I haven't started anything yet; I had to work late and just got home myself," she replied. "What would you like?"

"Something quick," said her husband. "I worked right through lunch so I could get home sooner."

"We could order pizza," said Tristen hopefully. "That's fast. And I wouldn't have to worry about which fork I ate with."

"Yeah, and I could take the pickup to get it. That would be even faster," added Kalani.

Both parents eyed their two sons in silence, their looks vetoing both suggestions.

"I've got chicken in the refrigerator. We can barbecue it on the back patio," said the boys' mom after a moment of silence.

"Good idea," said their dad. "Kal, you know how to fire up the grill. Start the coals burning while I get out of this uniform and into something more comfortable."

"And Tristen," added Tamala, as she headed with her husband for the bedroom to change her own clothes, "you can make a large bowl of salad so you can practice using that salad fork you love so much."

$$\text{5}$$

"Kalani, did you boys get over to the courthouse today with those papers?" asked their dad, as he sat back in his chair. On his plate were the remains of a chicken breast and a drumstick. But his pile of bones was dwarfed by the stack of bones on the plates of his two teenage sons.

"Yes, and Kalani put the receipt for filing them on the desk in your office," Tristen said. Kalani had not answered his father because he had a chicken leg in his mouth, still nibbling on it. The bone was picked clean, but Kalani was hoping to find an overlooked morsel missed in his hurry to finish everything on his plate before his brother finished his. They were in a race for the last piece of chicken. Kalani won because Tristen was slow eating his salad.

Putting his chicken leg down, Kalani wiped his mouth with his napkin. "We also got a list of all the notaries in the county. You were right; there's tons of them. Some of them have cell phones, so I'm going to call tonight to see if they notarized Mr. Granger's signature on a second will."

His dad nodded his head. "Just don't call after

seven o'clock. Evenings are family time, and I don't want you bothering people at night."

"Did Tristen tell you we got caught in that rainstorm today? I knew we should have taken the pickup to Aztec."

His dad nodded his head in silence. A smile played at the corners of his mouth, though, at Kalani's attempt to make him feel guilty about not letting him drive the truck.

"Yeah, we had to take cover in an old barn to keep from getting wet," said Tristen. "Kalani was afraid he was going to melt, but I told him that horse turds…"

"Not at the dinner table!" interrupted his mother with a stern look on her face.

Tristen looked contrite and went back to eating his salad.

"We met a boy who knew Wyatt Granger really well," said Kalani. "Wyatt lived next door before he moved in with the DeVilles. And he said Wyatt told him he was going to include him and his brother in his will."

Mason looked at Kalani with interest. "Really? What else did he tell you?"

Quickly Kalani told his dad about Dillon and Josh Gunderson and how they knew Wyatt Granger so well. He explained Wyatt's visit last Christmas when he mentioned his promise to leave the brothers some money but how they weren't included in the will when it was read.

"Did Dillon say if Wyatt ever made a second will?" asked Mason. "And if he did, where he put it?"

"No, the storm was over, and we had to hurry home before Mom got off work," said Kalani. "I'd like to talk to Dillon again and learn more about Mr. Granger. Maybe he told them about a second will."

"I'd like to speak with him as well," said his dad.

"Perhaps we could have the two brothers over for dinner," offered Tamala. "It sounds like they are barely scraping by. I'm sure they'd enjoy a good home-cooked meal."

"Yeah, I'm sure they would," said Kalani. "What if I run out to their home tomorrow and invite them over for dinner? I could take the pickup."

His father's scowl told him that he'd be on his bike again the next day.

∽

"Have another hamburger, Dillon," said Tamala Henderson. "There's plenty more."

"No thank you, ma'am," said Dillon Gunderson. "One is enough. I had a helping of potato salad and barbequed beans."

"I hope you're not holding back out of politeness," she said. "Kalani and Tristen have both had two burgers apiece, and I know Kalani will have another one."

"We're used to feeding hungry teenage boys," added Mason. "Trying to fill them up is like feeding a small, third-world country. I think they both have hollow legs they're trying to fill. And there's still plenty more patties on the grill."

Dillon smiled shyly at Mason and Tamala Henderson and went over to the platter of cooked patties keeping warm on the grill and started fixing another burger.

He and his brother Josh had accepted the invitation to dinner and were enjoying a relaxing meal of hamburgers grilled over a charcoal fire on the back patio of the Henderson home in the small village of Flora Vista.

As Dillon started his second burger, Mason said to him, "I understand Wyatt Granger used to live next door to you."

"Yes, sir, he did," replied Josh, answering for his younger brother who was chewing a mouthful of hamburger. "He was our neighbor for about two and a half years."

"Why did he move away from that house?"

"His nephew, Melvin, talked him into moving in with him and his family. Said it would be better to have a loving family to look after him in his old age."

"From what Kalani told me, it seems you two did a good job of looking after Wyatt while he was your neighbor," said Mason. "Didn't you nurse him back to health once?"

"Yes sir, we did, that first winter after he moved in next door. That's when we got to be such good friends with him."

"When was the last time you saw him?"

"A few days before Christmas. His nephew drove him out to our place so he could bring us some presents and everything for a big turkey dinner."

"Is that when Wyatt told you he planned to include the two of you in his will?"

"Yes sir, he did. But as soon as he did, his nephew got nervous and hustled him out of the house. It was almost like he didn't want him to talk about his will."

"Do you know if he ever made a second will?"

"No, not for sure," replied Josh, "but I don't think he did."

"Why do you say that?"

"He said that he was *thinking* of writing another one, like he would do it some time in the future. But a short time later, he was dead. I'm not sure he had enough time to do it."

"And if he did write it, did he have enough time to get a notary to witness his signature?" added Kalani in the silence that followed.

"When Wyatt visited you, how was his health?" said Mason. "Did he appear healthy enough to drive a car?"

"He seemed to be," said Josh, "but his nephew

was driving him around, and I don't think Uncle Wyatt was pleased about that. In fact, I got the impression that he wasn't happy living with the DeVilles at all."

"I heard that Mr. DeVille made him sell his car," said Dillon. His plate was empty again, his hamburger gone.

"It sounds like his nephew was very controlling of old man Granger," said Tristen.

"That's a very impolite way to refer to him," said his dad. "You call him Mr. Granger when you talk about him and show some respect, even if he is deceased."

"Yes sir," said Tristen, his voice humble.

"Even if Mr. Granger didn't have a car to drive," said Kalani, careful to use the polite form of the name, "he could have walked to a notary's. I saw one on my list who lived in the same neighborhood as the DeVille family. Papers don't have to be notarized at an office, do they, Pop?"

"That's right," said his dad, "papers can be notarized anywhere, just as long as the notary has his embossing machine to make it legal."

"But even if there was another will," said Tristen, "where would he have put it?"

"He could have hidden it somewhere," replied Kalani.

"Yeah, but where?" asked Tristen. "He didn't have a car anymore, so it would have to be hidden somewhere in the DeVille house. And if he did write another one, how would anyone know that it existed? Or where to look for it?"

"Maybe that's what he was trying to tell the nurse on his deathbed," said Kalani.

"Uncle Wyatt was always hiding things and then forgetting where he stashed them," said Josh in the pause that followed. "I remember once he forgot where he put my birthday present. He found it a week later and gave it to me late. It was a metric socket set, and I think about him every time I use it."

"I remember once he forgot where he put a check he got from the sale of some jewelry," added Dillon. "I helped him look for it. We searched all over. We finally found it in the book he had been reading. He had used it as a book marker and forgotten that he had done so."

"So, is it possible that he did write a second will, got it notarized, and then hid it somewhere in the DeVille's house?" asked Kalani. "All within that time between his visit to your place and when he died?"

Both Gunderson brothers shrugged their shoulders.

"Yeah, and if he did," said Tristen, "did the DeVilles find it and destroy it?"

"The only way to answer that," said Kalani, "is to find it."

He bit into his fourth hamburger as his dad quietly shook his head in amazement at his son's appetite.

Chapter 6
The Clue in the Food Court

"That was an easy shot, Kalani," said Danner. "Even Tristen could have made that. Why did you miss?"

"Guess my mind's not on basketball," Kalani replied. He chased the ball down the driveway of his house as it bounced toward the road.

"He's thinking about a second will," said Tristen, sitting in the shade of the Navajo Willow in front of the Henderson's house. "That's all he can talk about since the Gunderson brothers came over for hamburgers a couple of days ago."

"A second will?" asked Danner as Kalani passed him the ball.

"Yeah, a second one written by old man Granger," said Tristen. "I mean, Mr. Granger," he added quickly as his older brother glared at him.

"What makes you think Wyatt Granger wrote

another will?" Danner said. He drove past Kalani and made an easy shot.

"Just what you told us about him and how kind he was to his *Dineh* customers. And to Josh and Dillon Gunderson. I can't imagine him not leaving them something in his will."

"Not to mention the relatives who let him stay with them when he was so poor," added Danner as he caught the ball on the first bounce. "My grandmother was surprised when she heard they weren't in the will at all—just the DeVilles."

"And from what Josh and Dillon told us," said Tristen, "Wyatt promised he would leave them some of his fortune."

"How are you going to find out if there is another will?" asked Danner as he passed the ball to Kalani.

"I don't know," said Kalani. He put the basketball under one arm and wiped sweat off his forehead with the other. "I don't think the DeVilles will let me search their house. I just hope they haven't found it already and destroyed it."

"If one was ever written," added Tristen.

Kalani bounced the ball back to Danner without shooting a basket. "I'm not in the mood for basketball. And besides, it's too hot to be outside."

"Let's go to the mall and play video games at the

Fun Factory," said Danner. "We can all fit in the Rez Rocket."

"Shot gun!" said Kalani quickly.

∽

"Hey! I was on that machine!"

Kalani turned and saw a short kid walk over to a video game several machines down from where he stood watching his brother rack up a ton of points on the game he, Danner, and Tristen were playing. Standing at a machine down the row was Akron DeVille.

"That game's mine. I wasn't through playing it," continued the kid as he walked up to Akron.

Kalani didn't recognize him, and he figured that he was still in Middle School. He looked like he was only eleven or twelve years old.

Akron looked down at the shorter boy. "Beat it, kid," he said. "You left it, so it's mine now."

"I went to the bathroom. I left my cap on it to save it."

"You mean that one on the floor?" said Akron, giving a *Denver Rockies* baseball cap a kick.

Kalani watched the kid pick it up and dust it off. He placed it on his head and looked up at Akron. "That's my machine, and there were two games saved on it. You're playing one of my games!"

"Tough, kid. You left it, and I'm on it now. So, beat it!"

"I'm telling!" said the short kid. He stormed over to the cashier's counter and spoke to the teen working behind it.

"That kid is right," said Tristen to Kalani and Danner as he turned back to his own game. "I saw him put his cap on the machine and head for the bathroom."

"Akron must have tossed it to the floor when he saw two free games for the taking," said Kalani. "That would be just like him."

Kalani watched as the kid and a classmate of Kalani's who worked the front desk at the local hangout walked over to Akron. "This kid says that you're on his machine and playing his games," he said in a timid voice.

"He left it and I'm on it now," Akron replied, without looking up from his game.

"He said he left his cap on the machine to show he was still playing."

"There was no cap on it when I got here. It must have fallen off."

"He said that he put in enough money for two more games."

"There weren't any games on this when I came. Someone else must have played them and tossed his cap on the floor."

"Nuh uh," said the kid. "I wasn't gone that long." He looked up at the cashier who just stood there.

"He's right," said Kalani as he walked over to the three of them. "He wasn't gone but for a minute. Tristen saw him leave his cap on the machine to save it. There wasn't anyone else on it while he was in the bathroom."

"Butt out, dude," said Akron as he faced Kalani. "This is none of your business."

"Yes, it is," said Kalani, not backing down. "He was on this machine, and you took it from him while he was gone. Give it back to him."

Akron opened his mouth to say something, but he apparently changed his mind after seeing the look on Kalani's face. The cashier turned and hurried back to his station by the entrance.

"Here, cry baby. You can have it," said Akron as he hit the "off" button.

"Hey! I had two games saved on that!" said the kid. "You owe me for them."

"Pay him for his two games," said Kalani. His voice was slow, and his even tone never changed. He stared intently into Akron's eyes, their faces only inches apart.

"Here, punk," said Akron after he broke eye contact with Kalani. He slammed two tokens on the machine. "When I get rich, I'm going to buy this place and ban you from it!"

Then he turned to Kalani. "You watch your back,

dude. This isn't the last of this." And he slammed his shoulder into Kalani's as he headed for the door.

Kalani watched him leave the game arcade in silence, then rubbed his shoulder where Akron had bumped it.

Tristen walked over to Kalani as the kid put the tokens in the machine and started to play. "You want me to go jump Akron? I could put him in a guillotine for you if you want."

"No, he's not worth getting into trouble for," said Kalani. "Pop would ground you for fighting. No, a better revenge would be to find Wyatt's second will and watch Akron have to share his inheritance with someone else."

"That was pretty cool of you to stand up for that little kid," said Danner as the two brothers returned to the machine Danner was playing. "Not many people stand up to Akron DeVille."

"Well, he got me really angry the way he treated that kid," said Kalani. "I'm going to do everything I can to find that second will."

After a moment watching Danner try to score points, Kalani asked, "You two about through? I'm starved!"

"Not yet," said Danner. "We've still got another game to play, and your brother is beating the crap out of me! I'm not letting a freshman wrestler beat me! I'm the Rez Warrior after all. I always win!" He sighed in frustration as his turn came to an end.

"Only on a basketball court," said Tristen, moving to the machine to take his turn. "On this game, you're nothing but fresh meat." He smiled as he started scoring points.

"I'm going to head for the food court," said Kalani. "Come meet me there when you're through with your game."

Danner nodded his head in agreement. Tristen concentrated on racking up points.

Kalani left the Fun Factory where a lot of the kids in town came to play video games and headed for the area where all the food vendors were located. He had to go the full length of the mall since the two were at opposite ends of the building.

As he approached the food court, he heard a familiar voice ahead of him. It was Akron DeVille talking to his sister. Not wanting to provoke a confrontation in a crowded mall, Kalani was about to stop and let the twins get farther ahead of him when he heard Akron say, "the will."

Immediately Kalani was intrigued. The DeVille twins were talking about a will, and Kalani wanted to hear what they were saying.

He followed them into the food court and watched from a distance as they bought two slices of pizza. Going to another vendor, Kalani ordered a soft drink and followed the twins with his eyes as they headed for a table.

He wondered how he could get close enough

to overhear them without being noticed. He smiled when he saw them choose a table next to a very large pillar supporting the ceiling. The pillar was so large it would have taken him, Tristen, and Danner, all joining hands, to reach around it. There was an empty table on the opposite side of the pillar from where the DeVille twins were seated.

He quietly sat down at the empty table with his back to Akron and Tulsa. The pillar was big enough to block him from sight of the twins. Neither one was aware of him sitting so close, and he was able to easily overhear their conversation since they had to talk above a noisy crowd.

"You know that if there is another will, you won't get that Corvette you want so bad," said Tulsa. "Father heard old man Granger tell those Gunderson brothers he was going to leave them a lot of his money. There won't be enough for everyone if he did."

"True, *if* there is another will," replied Akron. "But nothing has turned up yet, and it's been almost six months since the old man died. Surely someone would have produced it by now if there was a second one."

"Then why's it taking the courts so long to decide we're the ones to get his money?"

"I don't know. I guess it just takes a long time to settle these things. Don't worry; old man Granger didn't write another will."

"I'm not so sure about that," said Tulsa. "It's

taking way too long. And people are beginning to ask if maybe there was a second one."

"Who's asking about another one?"

"Kalani Henderson for one," replied Tulsa. "A friend of mine who works at Dad's Diner overheard him and his father talking to the lawyer who helped old man Granger write his will. Kalani asked how the old man could write another one and make it be legal."

"There's no way he could have gone to the lawyer's office to make out another will. Father made old man Granger sell his car. And no one in the family ever drove him anywhere except to the bank and the pharmacy to refill his prescriptions."

"What about when the old man threw a hissy fit and demanded someone drive him around at Christmas time?" said Tulsa.

"Father was with the old geezer the whole time and made sure he didn't get a chance to give anyone anything but frozen turkeys and presents. Both you and I wrapped those presents, so we know there wasn't another will hidden in one of them."

"That's true," said Tulsa. "And I guess if the old man did slip a new will into one of those presents without us seeing it, whoever got it would have come forth by now."

"Right! So, stop worrying. There's no second will. The money will be ours soon enough."

About that time, Kalani saw Danner and Tristen

enter the food court and stop to scan the room for him. He hurriedly got up and headed toward them, careful to keep the bulky pillar between him and the DeVille twins. He could hardly wait to share what he had just learned.

Chapter 7
Kalani Turns Detective

"You're not going to believe what I just heard!" Kalani said as he steered Tristen and Danner toward a table on the other side of the food court. It was situated so that the large pillar still blocked the view of the three teens from the DeVille twins. Kalani seated himself at their table so that he faced the pillar. If the twins spotted him and headed toward him, he could change the conversation to something other than what he was about to tell his friends.

"I just overhead Akron and Tulsa talking about a second will," Kalani said softly.

"What did they say?" asked Tristen. Both he and Danner leaned forward to hear Kalani over the loud background noise of the food court.

"Tulsa thinks that there might be another will," said Kalani. "But Akron is sure there isn't."

Kalani paused as he recalled the conversation he had just overheard.

"They also said that their dad forced Wyatt Granger to sell his car. And that he always drove him around on his errands."

"Why would Mr. DeVille make him sell his car?" asked Danner. "That would make him a burden on whoever had to drive him somewhere."

"I think he wanted to keep him isolated from other people," said Kalani. "Akron said no one took him anywhere except to the bank and the pharmacy. It sounded like Wyatt had to get forceful with Melvin just to be driven around to deliver Christmas presents."

"I know my aunt who took care of Wyatt said he wasn't too feeble to drive," said Danner. "His eyesight was still good, and his mind was still sharp. She was surprised he agreed to turn in his license and give up driving."

"It sounds like Melvin was very controlling of Mr. Granger," said Tristen. "I feel for him; I know what it's like to have someone tell you what you can and can't do all the time."

"That's because you're so scatter-brained," said Kalani. "If Mom and Pop didn't watch you like a hawk, you'd never get your chores done. Or your homework. Sometimes I think the only reason you know your name is because they yell it at you all the time."

"No, not Mom and Pop," said Tristen. "I meant *you!*"

"*I* don't boss you around," said Kalani.

"Yes, you do. You're always telling me what to do."

"You two stop arguing," said Danner. "This isn't getting us anywhere." Turning to Kalani he asked, "What else did you overhear them say?"

"They are not sure if another will was written," said Kalani. "If there is one, it hasn't turned up yet. No one has come forward with it, and the DeVilles haven't found anything at their house. But they are still worried about there being another will and having to share Wyatt's wealth with others."

"So, it's a dead end then," said Tristen.

"No, I'm still certain that Wyatt Granger wrote another will. I've just got to find where he hid it."

"How are you going to do that? There aren't any more leads to follow."

"I don't know," said Kalani. "I think I should talk to the nephew and niece who took Wyatt in from time to time. They might know something about another will."

About that time Kalani looked up and saw Akron and Tulsa DeVille leaving the food court through a door on the far side of the room.

"Come on you two. Let's get something to eat," said Kalani, standing up and heading for the food counters. Then turning to his brother, he added, "but don't order anything that takes a long time to fix. I want to get out of here and go home to talk to Pop. I want to tell him what I've learned. He might have some ideas about what to do next."

"See, I told you he bosses me around," said Tristen to Danner.

Danner just shook his head.

5

"What did you two do today?" asked Mason Henderson as he sat at the dinner table. "Nothing too reckless, I hope."

"No, we just went to the Fun Factory in the mall with Danner," said Tristen. "I beat him four games out of five at *Hot Shot Basketball*."

"Yeah, that's the only way you'll beat him in basketball," said Kalani with a grin. "In a video game."

"That's because I'm not a giraffe like he is. Or you!"

Their father chuckled at his younger son's comments. At six foot three, Kalani towered over both his mother and father. And he still had two years of high school to grow some more.

"And Kalani almost got into a fight with Akron DeVille," continued Tristen.

Their father's smile changed to a stern look, and he stared at his oldest son.

"Don't worry, Pop. I didn't throw any punches," Kalani said in a hurry. "I just stood up for a little kid. Akron got on the kid's machine when he went to the bathroom and played his games. I just made him get off and let the kid have it back."

"And he made Akron give the kid two tokens for the games he used up," added Tristen, his voice filled with pride.

Mason's face relaxed. "Well, I'm glad I didn't have to go to the jail to bail you out for being a public disturbance. You would really have been in trouble."

Kalani nodded his head solemnly. He had never gotten into any trouble that involved the police. He couldn't imagine what his father would do to him if he did. And he didn't want to find out either.

In an effort to change the subject, Kalani quickly added, "I also overheard Akron and Tulsa talking about a second will of Mr. Granger."

"What did they say?" his father asked.

Kalani told his father what he had learned from the overheard conversation of the twins. He finished by saying, "I still think there's another will out there. But I don't know where it could be hidden or how I can locate it."

"You still want to find it?" asked Tamala Henderson.

"Yeah, especially after getting to know Dillon and Josh. They deserve to inherit some of Mr. Granger's estate."

"That's true," said their mother. "I was impressed with how nice they were when we had them over for hamburgers."

"But I have no way of knowing how I would find another will unless I talked to the other relatives that took Mr. Granger in," said Kalani. "Do you think I should, Pop?"

Mason paused for a moment before answering his son. "Yes, you could interview his other relatives. But I wouldn't get my hopes up if I were you. Detective work is long, hard, and arduous. You might not find out anything more than what you already know."

"Yeah, I know," Kalani said. "But I've got an expert I can always ask if I get stumped."

"Who's that?" asked his father.

"You," said Kalani, a big smile on his face. "You always solve the mystery you're investigating."

"Not always," said his father, a pleased look on his face at his son's flattery. "There were quite a few cases still open back in Houston that I didn't solve before I retired. And sometimes, mysteries never get solved, even with an entire police force working on them."

"And you be careful around those DeVille twins," said their mother. "They won't like the fact you're looking for another will. And neither will their father, Melvin. I don't want to have to take you to the hospital because you've been fighting the whole family."

"Oh, I'm not afraid of Akron DeVille," said Kalani. "Or his dad. If he tries to get belligerent with me, I'll sic Tristen on him. His guillotines hurt."

Tristen beamed with pride at the unexpected compliment.

Chapter 8
Discouraging Conversations

Bright and early the next morning, Kalani and his brother got on their motorcycles and headed down the Old Aztec Highway. For years, this narrow, two lane road following the Animas River had been the main road between Aztec and Farmington with the little village of Flora Vista sitting halfway between them. Then, about 20 years ago, a newer, bigger highway was built, one farther away from the river and without as many twists and turns. It provided a straighter, more direct link between the three towns but had demoted the old highway to a backwater country road.

Driving down the older but more picturesque road, Kalani enjoyed the scenery as he and Tristen passed by large, country haciendas and open pastures with cattle grazing in them. Midway between their home in Flora Vista and the city limits of Aztec, the boys turned into the lane leading down toward the river and the house of Dillon and Josh Gunderson.

As Kalani rode down the hundred yards of dirt lane leading to the Gunderson home, he noticed how old and shabby the house appeared. There were several areas on the roof of the house where shingles had blown off, exposing the black tarpaper underneath that waterproofed the building. The wood siding on the outside was in desperate need of fresh paint. A lot of the wood trim around the windows was cracked and split, needing to be replaced.

The barn next to the house where he and Tristen had taken shelter from the storm was in even worse condition. The roof actually had gaping holes in it, and the outside walls had gaps showing where several planks were missing. The remaining boards were so old and faded Kalani couldn't tell its original color.

As Kalani and Tristen pulled up to the house, Dillon and Josh came out from the barn, wiping their hands on old, dirty, red, garage rags.

"What brings you two back here?" asked Dillon, extending his hand. "Is there another storm on the horizon that I can't see? Or did one of you run out of gas again?"

Kalani shook the proffered hand and laughed, "No, we're here to ask you about Wyatt Granger."

"Well, you know he doesn't live next door anymore," said Dillon.

Tristen looked at him puzzled. Kalani snorted

at the humor. He noticed the change in Dillon from when they had first taken shelter in his barn. Kalani saw that an evening spent eating hamburgers with the Henderson family had relaxed Dillon to the point that he was no longer shy and could even joke with Kalani and Tristen.

"We'd like to ask you some more questions about what Wyatt said to you when he was here last Christmas."

"Let's go back in the barn," Josh said to his brother. "We can talk while we finish working on that engine. The owner is coming over this afternoon to pick it up, and we've got a lot more to do before he gets here."

Kalani and Tristen followed the brothers back inside the barn to the makeshift work bench where a small motorcycle motor was disassembled. As Josh and Dillon got back to the task at hand, Kalani noticed how well they worked together as a team. Dillon held the flashlight for his brother and seemed to anticipate what he needed and often handed him tools and engine parts without Josh saying a word.

"What exactly did Wyatt tell you when he was here the last time you saw him?" asked Kalani.

Josh continued to work on the small engine as his younger brother began to speak. "He came to the house the day before Christmas Eve about midafternoon. He had a turkey and a bag of groceries for us. He also had two wrapped Christmas gifts."

"They were new coats," said Josh without looking up from his work. "We really needed them too, but then, Uncle Wyatt always seemed to know what we needed."

"Yeah, that's right," said Dillon. "Uncle Wyatt apologized that his gifts weren't all that much. But he promised our inheritance from him would be much more. He said it would get us started in our own business. I figured it would be enough to send Josh to San Juan College to take their classes on small engine repair."

"But his nephew, Melvin, got really jumpy when Wyatt started talking about his will," said Josh, still working on the engine in front of him. "I got the impression Melvin didn't like him talking to us about it."

"Yes, Melvin was driving him around that day," said Dillon. "And when the conversation turned to what he was going to leave us, Melvin practically tossed Uncle Wyatt out the front door, saying that they had more stops to make before dark."

"Did Wyatt ever say that he had made out a second will?" asked Kalani.

"No," Dillon said aloud as Josh silently shook his head. "He only said 'his will' when he spoke about it. I assumed there was only one. And when it was read by the lawyer after he died, we weren't mentioned at all."

"Then why haven't the DeVilles gotten their money yet?" asked Tristen.

"It still has to go through probate," said Josh without stopping his work on the engine.

"What's that?" asked Tristen.

"That's the court system that handles wills and inheritances," said Josh.

"Does it always take this long to settle an inheritance?" asked Kalani.

"I don't know," said Josh. "I've never inherited anything before."

"Did he say if he was going to include anyone else in his will?" said Kalani.

"No, as soon as the topic came up, Melvin hurried Uncle Wyatt into the car and off they drove," said Dillon.

"I wonder if his other relatives would know anything about it," said Kalani. "What were their names again?"

"His niece is Kaylee Carey, and his nephew is Riley Quigley," said Dillon. "They both live in Aztec."

"Maybe we should go and talk with them," said Kalani. "Do you know where they live?"

Both Dillon and Josh nodded their heads yes. After Kalani Googled the directions to their houses on his cell phone, he and his brother took their leave of Josh and Dillon. As they headed up the lane toward the road to Aztec, Kalani redoubled his determination to find Wyatt Granger's second will and help the two brothers open their own repair shop.

∽

Kalani and Tristen pulled up to a small house in Aztec on their motorcycles. As they stopped by the curb, they saw a tall, muscular young man a couple of years older than Kalani lifting weights in the garage. The garage door was up to provide ventilation, but even in the open air, his body was covered in sweat.

The muscular man saw the two stop in front of his house, but he finished his set before he put the barbell on the garage floor. Walking out, he met the Henderson brothers in the middle of his driveway.

"Are you Riley Quigley?" asked Kalani as he walked up to him.

"Yeah, I'm Riley," he said, offering his hand. "What can I do for you?"

"I'm Kalani Henderson, and this is my brother, Tristen."

Even though Kalani was three inches taller, he wasn't sure that he wanted to shake Riley's hand. The young man was powerfully built, almost outweighing both the brothers together, and the muscles of his arm writhed like a python squeezing its prey when he extended his hand in greeting. But Kalani's politeness, learned from his strict father, compelled him to take the proffered hand. He regretted it as soon as he did. Riley's grip told him the muscular young man worked hard doing manual labor. And he used his hands a lot!

Tristen thrust his hands into the pockets of his shorts to avoid the painful politeness his brother had just undergone.

"We would like to ask you about your uncle, Wyatt Granger," said Kalani, shaking the pain out of his squeezed hand after Riley released it. "I understand he used to live with you sometimes?"

"Yeah, he did," said Riley, heading back to the garage. "Why are you asking about him?"

Kalani and Tristen followed him into the shady interior.

"We heard about your uncle from Josh and Dillon Gunderson. Do you know them?" said Kalani.

Riley nodded his head as he picked up the barbell and started doing bicep curls again. "They're the two boys who lived next door to Uncle Wyatt."

"They told us when Mr. Granger visited them Christmas Eve, he mentioned he wanted to include them in his will," said Kalani. "But after he died, they weren't mentioned in it at all. Did he ever talk to you about leaving anyone other than Melvin his money?"

Riley finished his set and put the barbell on the floor. "Yes, he did, in fact. He said something about a second will last Christmas when Melvin was driving him around and he brought me a Christmas present."

"I *knew* it!" said Kalani to Tristen, a smug look on his face.

"Knew what?" asked Riley.

"That there was another will."

"But did he actually write another one?" Tristen asked his brother. "Didn't he die sometime around Christmas? Did he have enough time to write a will and get a rotatory republic to witness it?"

"You mean a notary public," said Kalani with a sigh.

"Yeah," answered Tristen, "that's what I said."

"When did Wyatt Granger die?" Kalani asked Riley.

"It was a week after Christmas, on New Year's Eve," he answered. "I remember because I missed a New Year's Eve party."

"Were you there at the hospital when he died?"

"No, I got there too late. When I got the call from his caretaker that Uncle Wyatt wanted to see me, I went to Melvin's house thinking that's where he would be. When I got there, Melvin told me Uncle Wyatt had been taken by ambulance to the hospital."

"Didn't Melvin and his family go with him to the hospital?" asked Tristen. "If Kalani were in the hospital, my parents and I would be there with him."

"Melvin and his wife were throwing a big New Year's Eve party for some of the wealthy, upper crust people of San Juan County and didn't want to cancel it because Uncle Wyatt was hospitalized," answered Riley. "I couldn't believe how cold they were to Uncle Wyatt being so ill he had to go to the emergency room. When I finally got there, he had already died. His Navajo caretaker was doing something with his shoes as I came into the room."

"So, you weren't there when Wyatt tried to tell the nurse something in her ear?" said Kalani.

"Tell her what?" asked Riley as he picked up the barbell for another set of curls.

"No one knows," said Kalani. "I personally think he was trying to tell her where a second will was. But he was too weak to get it out."

"That would make sense," said Riley, setting the barbell down after his set. Kalani noticed that the man's arms were pumped and swollen, almost as big as his leg.

"Why do you say that it makes sense to you?" said Kalani.

"Because Uncle Wyatt was really meticulous in his business dealings. He might be carefree about giving away his money to others in need. And he might be forgetful about unimportant stuff, but he was very careful about keeping precise records of his finances. It makes sense that if he wrote a second will, he would put it somewhere safe."

"So, you think it's possible that he did write a second will?" asked Kalani.

"Yeah, I guess. Uncle Wyatt promised that he would take care of me in his will since I and my cousin Kaylee took turns caring for him when he was broke. But I wasn't mentioned at all when the will was read."

"Why didn't he just live with you all the time?" asked Tristen. "Why bounce back and forth between you and your cousin?"

"I work in the oil field as a floor hand," said Riley. "When there are wells to drill, work is plentiful, and the money is good. But when there is no drilling to do, I get laid off, and the money dries up. When that happens and I have to leave New Mexico to find work, Uncle Wyatt moves in with Kaylee and her husband. Or I should say, that's what he used to do when that happened."

"And since you weren't mentioned in Wyatt's will, there must have been a second one written," said Kalani, more to himself.

Riley shrugged his shoulders. "I guess so."

"Do you have any idea where he might have hidden a second will?" asked Kalani.

"No, I have no clue. Even though he lived with me, I didn't know him that well since my work often kept me out in the oil field for days on end."

"I wonder if your cousin, Kaylee, would know more about another will," said Kalani.

"She might," said Riley. "The two of them were pretty close."

After verifying Kaylee's address and thanking Riley for his help, Kalani again went through the torture of another bone-crushing handshake with the muscular nephew of Wyatt Granger.

Chapter 9
The Grocery Store Clue

Kalani flipped on his turn signal, checked his
rear-view mirrors, and moved into the right-hand lane
of the main highway between Aztec and Farmington.
He watched his brother follow behind him. Up ahead
he spotted the sign for County Road 2138 and saw
where it met the highway. He turned off the highway
and on to the county road, driving slowly, looking for
number 5 on the mailboxes lining the dirt road. He
found it in front of a small mobile home with a short
chain-link fence around the front yard.

He stopped, turned off the motor, removed his
helmet, and waited as Tristen pulled up beside him.
As soon as his brother had killed the engine of his
motorbike, Kalani whacked him on the shoulder, hard.

"What was that for?" asked Tristen, rubbing his
shoulder.

"You didn't use your turn signal when you
changed lanes back there," said Kalani. He whacked

him again. "And that's for not using it when you turned off the highway and on to the county road."

"Ouch!" said Tristen. He held his shoulder and leaned away from his brother, least he find another reason to whack him. "Okay, I get it. Use my turn signals."

"You're lucky it wasn't Pop riding with you. He would have given you your first ticket." Kalani stepped off his bike and fastened his helmet to it. "And made you work outdoors in the hot sun pulling weeds to pay for it."

Walking up to the front door of the trailer, Kalani knocked. He waited patiently for a few moments, but hearing nothing, he knocked again, a little harder.

"You will have to let yourself in," he heard a faint voice say. "I can't make it to the door."

Kalani opened the door slowly and looked in. He saw a portion of a darkened living room with an old TV on a rickety stand with a soccer game on the screen. Opening the door wider, he walked in and saw a couch against the opposite wall from the TV. As his eyes adjusted to the darkness of the room, he heard a loud thump. Turning toward the sound, he saw a young man about twenty years old with a cast on his leg clumsily lower his foot to the floor with his two hands.

"Hi, I'm Kalani Henderson, and I'm looking for Kaylee Carey," he said going farther into the room. "I'd like to talk to her about her uncle, Wyatt Granger."

"I'm Kilian, her husband," said the young man with the cast. "She went to the pharmacy to refill a prescription for me." He grimaced as he moved his leg a bit to face Kalani better.

"What happened to your leg?" asked Tristen who had followed his brother inside and stood looking at the man on the couch.

"I tore the ligaments in my knee playing flag football," said Kilian.

"I didn't think flag football was so dangerous," said Tristen with a serious look on his face. "I play football and haven't hurt my knees at all. Thought regular football was tougher than flag."

"It is, usually. But I guess I zigged when I should have zagged. I was trying to juke my way to the goal line when I injured my knee."

"Did it hurt when you did it?"

"No, I didn't feel anything except for a slight twinge," said Kilian. "The real damage was done when I kept playing on it for two more hours."

"It didn't hurt at all while you were playing on it?" asked Tristen.

Kilian shrugged his shoulders. "Just a little, but I told myself to stop being such a wimp. And so, I kept on playing."

"What did the doctor say when you went to see him?"

"That the ACL was badly torn and that I needed surgery to correct it." Kilian sighed as he said this.

"When is your surgery scheduled?" asked Kalani.

"It's not scheduled yet," answered Kilian. "I have to wait until I've been on my job for six months before I'm covered by insurance."

"When will the six months be up?"

"I've got three more to go."

"Won't you lose your job if you can't go to work for three months?"

"They put me on desk duty," said Kilian. "I answer the phone and do all the paperwork of running a fire station until my surgery."

"Yuck! Three months stuck behind a desk," said Kalani. "I would go crazy if I had to stay sitting down all day long."

"Yes, just sitting around is torture, but at least I've got a job. Our finances would really be hurting if I wasn't working."

Kalani looked around discreetly and saw how humble the mobile home was. It was small and simple, and the living room didn't contain much in the way of furniture, just a couch and the small TV on its wobbly stand. In the kitchen area he could make out a simple wooden table with three mismatched chairs around it. The furniture was old-fashioned and reminded him of his grandmother's home. Kalani figured Kilian and Kaylee had bought their furnishings at a yard sale or else inherited them as hand-me-downs.

As the thought of inheriting hit Kalani, he remembered the purpose of his visit.

"We'd like to ask your wife about her uncle," said Kalani. "Will she be back soon?"

"I hope so," said Kilian. "My knee is killing me. I need another pain pill."

All three turned toward the front door as they heard the sound of a vehicle driving up on the gravel driveway in front of the trailer. A minute later, the door opened and in stepped a short, dark haired young woman in her early twenties. Kalani could see a strong resemblance to her cousin, Riley Quigley.

"Hi honey, how are you feeling?" she asked going directly to her husband on the couch and handing him a small paper bag. "Does your knee hurt much?" She ignored the two boys in the room, concentrating instead on her injured husband.

"No, it's not hurting much at all," said Kilian.

But to Kalani, the grimace on Kilian's face told him he was suffering quite a lot of pain. Kalani could well understand how the young man had played football for two hours on an injured knee.

Evidently his wife saw through his bravado as well, because she hurried into the kitchen and got a glass of water for her husband. He already had the bag opened and the cap off the small medicine bottle when she handed him the glass. He popped a pill into his mouth and swallowed it with a gulp of water. He then gingerly grabbed his leg and gently lifted it back on the couch and reclined.

Kalani turned to the wife who was watching her husband with concern.

"Hi, Kaylee, I'm Kalani Henderson, and this is my brother, Tristen," he said. "Could we ask you about your uncle, Wyatt Granger?"

Kaylee turned to the two and nodded. "Did you know Uncle Wyatt?" she asked.

"No, not directly," said Kalani. "But we've heard a lot about him, especially from Josh and Dillon Gunderson."

"And your cousin Riley," added Tristen.

"Yeah, they all thought it might be a good idea to talk to you about your uncle," said Kalani.

"What do you want to know about Uncle Wyatt?" asked Kaylee.

"Did he ever mention writing a second will?" said Kalani.

"Yes, he did," answered Kilian from the couch. "In fact, I saw it."

"You saw a second will?" asked Kalani astonished, turning toward the couch. "When? Where?"

"Kaylee and I were in the supermarket the morning of New Year's Eve buying groceries when we ran into Uncle Wyatt. He was heading for the pharmacy," said Kilian.

"Why was he carrying his will around in a grocery store?" asked Tristen with a puzzled face.

"I don't know," Kilian answered. "He asked if we had enjoyed the turkey he had given us for Christmas.

We told him 'yes' but that we had finished all the food he brought over and were restocking the kitchen."

"But how did the subject of his will come up?" asked Tristen.

Kalani elbowed his brother in the ribs. "Let him finish," he said.

Kilian continued. "He looked into our grocery cart and said that we didn't have much. I explained the little we had in the basket was going to have to last us for a week. I was still looking for a job with one of the fire departments in the area, but no one was hiring until after the new year started. We were trying to stretch what little money we had until Kaylee got her next paycheck from the jewelry store where she works part-time."

"That's when Uncle Wyatt opened his wallet and handed us each a hundred-dollar bill," said Kaylee when her husband stopped. The grimace on Kilian's face told Kalani that the pain medication hadn't kicked in yet.

"A folded-up sheet of paper fell out when he did that," continued Kaylee as her husband adjusted his leg on the couch. "When Kilian picked it up and returned it, Uncle Wyatt said it was another will that would take care of all our money problems. He even said that he planned to cut my cousin, Melvin out of the inheritance."

"Did you actually see that written in the will?" asked Kalani, his eyes wide with surprise.

"No, the will was folded up really small so it would fit in his wallet," Kilian said. "I couldn't see what was written."

"But he definitely said it was another will?" said Kalani.

"Yes," Kilian answered. "He said he wrote it himself. I asked him if it was legal. He replied his lawyer told him it would be legal if his signature were notarized by someone not in the will."

"Did he say anything else about it?"

"Only that he was going to put it somewhere where no one could get to it without legal authority."

"I wonder where that would be?" said Tristen.

"I wanted to ask him the same thing," said Kaylee, "but about that time Melvin stormed into the store looking for Uncle Wyatt. He started shouting at him, wanting to know what was taking so long in getting a simple prescription filled."

"What happened next?" asked Tristen. "Did your husband punch him in the mouth? I would have!"

Kalani again elbowed his brother in the ribs.

"Well, I *would* have," Tristen said. "That man was mean to old man Granger." Then looking at his brother's face, "I mean Mr. Granger," he added hurriedly, moving out of the way of another jab in the ribs.

"Melvin was making such a scene in public that Kilian and I hurriedly said good-bye to Uncle Wyatt and went back to shopping. A few minutes later, I saw

Melvin and Uncle Wyatt as they left the store. Melvin was still chewing my uncle out, big time. I really felt sorry for him. I was glad, too, that Melvin was being cut off from any inheritance, even though he's my cousin."

"Now, if we can only find where your uncle hid that paper," said Tristen.

"It has to be somewhere nearby," said Kalani. "He died later that same day, didn't he?"

"Yes," said Kaylee. "The incident at the grocery store happened New Year's Eve day. That night the ambulance took him to the hospital where he died."

"I wonder how we can find out where your cousin took your uncle after they left the store. Wherever that is, that's where the will is hidden."

After a pause to think, he added, "Guess we'll have to ask one of the DeVilles directly."

"Good luck with that," said Tristen, "especially after what you made Akron do in the Fun Factory."

Kalani's face fell at his brother's comment.

Chapter 10
A Navajo Taco Dinner

"Is there anything else you can recall from when you ran into Wyatt at the grocery store?" Kalani asked the married couple. "Did anything else happen? Did he say anything more before your cousin Melvin showed up?"

"I just remember the papers falling out of his wallet," answered Kilian from the couch.

"Papers?" said Kalani. "I thought you said the will was just one sheet of paper, all folded up small to fit in his wallet."

"Yeah, that's true, and Wyatt told us it was his will," said Kilian. "But a small slip of paper fell out with it. It was just big enough to have a few letters on it, H-0-Z-H-0 with an accent over the second '0'."

"Hozhò?" asked Tristen. "Is that a word?"

"It could be," said Kilian. "It may be Navajo. Their words have lots of accents in them. I noticed it when I handed it back to Wyatt."

"Your uncle was pretty fluent in Navajo, right?" Kalani asked Kaylee.

"Yes, from years of owning a trading post on the Rez."

"I wonder why he would have a *Dineh* word in his wallet?"

"Maybe it was a new word and he wanted to remember it," said Kilian looking up at his visitors from where he lay on the couch. Kalani noticed that his speech was slower and beginning to slur. Evidently the pain medication was starting to take some effect.

"Did he say anything else before Melvin arrived?" Kalani asked the couple. "Did he mention where they were headed after the store?"

Both Kilian and Kaylee shook their heads.

"Oh man, you're killing me!" said Kalani with a sigh. "There is only one way to find out if Wyatt went somewhere else and hid his will before going home."

As the three others in the room looked at Kalani expectedly, he continued, "Well d'uh! It's obvious. I have to ask Melvin himself where he took Wyatt after they left the grocery store."

About that time, Kalani heard the soft chimes of *Westminster Quarters*, the tune of Big Ben, the famous clock in London, ringing from behind him. Turning around, he saw a clock hanging on the kitchen wall, and he stared at it. He watched, with his mouth open in surprise, as the two hands spun rapidly around the clock's face. In a matter of thirty seconds, he watched the clock advance six hours and stop with the hands indicating two o'clock in the afternoon.

"Oh, that's the atomic clock Uncle Wyatt gave us," said Kilian slurring his words. "He said he had one just like it at home and loved it. I guess he figured we would like one too."

He stopped and frowned as a quick spasm of pain hit his knee. After a moment, his pain lessened and he continued, "I had just replaced the battery in it when you knocked. It had stopped, and the time was wrong."

"I wondered why you took so long to answer the door," Kalani said. "We have a clock at home that's hard to change when the time gets out of whack." He paused and grinned. "I usually make Tristen reset it when it's wrong."

"This clock does it itself," said Kilian, slurring his words even more. "It adjusts automatically. It picks up a radio signal. From the NIST Laboratory. It's in Boulder, Colorado."

He giggled and continued, "It's funny to watch. The hands spin around fast. Like in a corny movie. Showing time passing."

"When did Wyatt give you that clock?" said Kalani.

"Last Christmas," said Kaylee for her husband. His face winced with more pain in spite of the medication. "We had just gotten married, and it was a wedding present."

Kilian interrupted his wife, "And he said every new home needs a kitchen clock. So, the cook can burn the beans." Then grinning at his wife, he added, "But my wife doesn't need a clock to burn beans. She knows how already."

Kaylee grabbed a pillow from behind her husband's head as he lay on the couch and hit him with it. "Just for that, I *will* burn your dinner tonight."

Kilian giggled.

∽

Driving home down the picturesque Old Aztec Highway, Kalani didn't pay attention to the pastoral scenery passing by him. Instead, he thought about what he had just learned about Wyatt Granger.

That he was generous and compassionate was evident from the way he had treated his Navajo customers allowing them to trade their jewelry for groceries. Or how he had promised to remember his relatives and the Gunderson brothers in his will for taking care of him when he was poor and sick. To Kalani, it seemed Wyatt must have realized his first will was a mistake and had changed his mind about leaving all his money to the self-centered Melvin.

Kalani was now sure another will had been

written which included Josh and Dillon, and the cousins Riley and Kaylee. Additionally, from what he had overheard from Akron and Tulsa DeVille, he was convinced it had not been found and destroyed.

But on the other hand, Kalani didn't know if the second will had been notarized and made legal. If it had been, then where was it hidden? Because Kaylee's husband had seen it the very day Wyatt died, it had to be located somewhere in the DeVille house or at some location visited by Wyatt after leaving the grocery store. And since Melvin had been the only one with him on his errands, he alone knew where Wyatt Granger had gone after running into Kaylee and Kilian that fateful day. How Kalani was going to find out that bit of information, he had no idea.

ꙅ

Kalani was surprised to see the Rez Rocket parked in front of his house when he and Tristen pulled up on their motorcycles. As they put them in the garage, Danner got out of his pickup.

"You didn't have to wait out front in the hot sun for us to show up," said Kalani as he walked up to his friend. "You could have gone to the patio in back and waited in the shade."

"No, that's not done," said Danner. "*Dineh* wait in their vehicle until whoever they are visiting comes out and invites them in. I once waited over an hour for my aunt to invite me and my grandmother inside her hogan. We sat in my pickup until she came out and told us she was ready for us to come in."

"What's a hogan?" asked Kalani.

"It's a traditional Navajo dwelling," said Danner. "It's hexagonal with six sides, and the entrance always faces east, towards the rising sun. It usually has a dirt floor, and the roof is simply sod laid over small tree branches."

"Aren't people allowed to come in them?"

"Yes," said Danner. "but not until invited in. The *Dineh* value their privacy, even from their relatives. If you show up unexpectedly, whoever you're visiting might not be ready to receive you."

"Well, come on inside our hogan, and I'll get you something cold to drink. You must be hot and thirsty."

A few minutes later Kalani handed his friend a tall glass of iced tea already sweetened with sugar, "sweet tea" his Texas raised parents called it.

"I wasn't expecting you today," Kalani said as his friend finished the iced tea in one gulp. "Are you here to get beat in Rez ball again?" he added as he refilled Danner's glass.

"No, I was hoping to sell you guys tickets to a Navajo Taco dinner," Danner said. He finished the second glass of tea almost as quickly as the first one. "I'm selling them for my sister to go to a camp down by Crownpoint."

"A Navajo Taco?" asked Tristen. "I thought tacos were Mexican food, not Navajo."

"It's a large piece of fry bread with lettuce, tomato, onion, and ground beef on it, all covered with taco sauce. It's about the size and shape of a medium pizza."

"Sounds good," said Tristen. "When is the dinner?"

"In a couple of weeks at the Shiprock Chapter house. If I sell ten more tickets, Sequoia will have enough money to go to the camp."

"A Chapter house?" asked Tristen. "What's that? A part of a book?"

Danner laughed at his question. "No, it's how the Navajo Reservation is divided up. Just like New Mexico is divided into counties, the Navajo Nation is divided into chapters. It's the local government on the Rez."

"Oh, I see," said Tristen. "Well, I'm sure Mom and Pop will buy four tickets from you since it's for a good cause. Besides, I've never had a Navajo Taco, and I want to try one."

"Wait a minute," said Kalani. "This gives me an idea. Do you have the tickets with you now?"

"Yeah, they're in my truck."

"This may be the excuse I've been looking for to talk to Melvin about where he took Wyatt Granger the day he died."

At Danner's puzzled look, Kalani explained what

he had learned from his visit with Riley Quigley and Kilian and Kaylee Carey.

"Dropping by the DeVille house to sell tickets to a fund raiser will give me the perfect chance to chat with Melvin and maybe find out what happened to Wyatt that afternoon," said Kalani as he finished his explanation of the day's events. "I'm sure I can casually steer the conversation to his uncle and how he died suddenly."

"When are you planning on going over?" asked Tristen.

"Right now, since Danner has the tickets in the Rez Rocket."

"But what if no one is home? We'll have wasted our time. And gas."

"Then I'll do the *Dineh* wait-till-invited-in trick in their front yard."

He paused, then added, "I wish Pop would let me drive his pickup. It's going to be really hot sitting in the scorching sun on a motorcycle if no one's home."

Chapter 11
A Successful Visit

"What makes you think I would drive all the way to Shiprock for a Navajo Taco?" said Corella DeVille.

Kalani and Tristen were standing in the entrance hall of her house and had just explained the purpose of their visit.

"But it's for a good cause," said Kalani. "It is so Sequoia Yazzie can go to a camp later this summer."

"I don't care if it is," she replied. "We don't have the money to spend on such foolishness."

About that time, the front door flew open and in stormed the DeVille twins.

"I *thought* those were your motorcycles in our driveway," exploded Akron. "What are you doing here?"

"We're selling tickets to a Navajo Taco dinner in Shiprock," said Kalani, calmly looking his classmate in the eye. "It's so a young girl can go to a summer camp in Crownpoint."

"I'll bet she's Navajo, isn't she?" said Tulsa.

"Yes, it's Danner Yazzie's younger sister."

"Why do you think we would want to help that family out?" said Akron. "They live on the Rez and don't pay rent. I'm sure they have enough money to pay for her camp without mooching off of people like us."

"Yes," said Mrs. DeVille. "Tell her to ask her aunt for the money. We certainly paid her enough to take care of that old man when he was alive."

"Besides," added Tulsa with a toss of her hair, "someone might see us there with all those Navajos and tell everyone that we were Indian lovers. That would completely ruin my reputation at school."

Tristen's mouth flew open. He had never heard such blatant prejudice in all his young life.

Kalani's jaw muscles twitched as he clamped his mouth shut. It was all he could do to keep the anger out of his voice.

Akron opened the front door wider, indicating that the Henderson brothers were to leave. "Get your motorcycles off our property before the neighbors see them. They're going to think we're too poor to drive cars."

Silently Kalani and Tristen turned to leave. Just at that moment Melvin appeared in the doorway.

"Whose bikes are those in the driveway?" he asked. "I had to park on the street because they're blocking the garage."

"Sorry sir," answered Kalani. "They're ours. We were here to sell tickets to a Navajo Taco fund raiser. We were only planning to be here for a moment. We'll move them right away."

"A fund raiser, you say?" said Melvin. Turning to his wife he asked, "How many did you buy?"

"None," she answered with a sneer. "We don't have the money to waste on *those* kinds of people."

"Actually, we do," he said. "I just came from the lawyer's, and old Wyatt's will should be finalized in about a week. Then we will have plenty of money to spend however we see fit."

Turning to Kalani he asked, "How many tickets do you have? And how much are they?"

"I've got six tickets left. They're ten dollars apiece."

"I'll take all six of them. And here's a hundred dollars for them."

"But I don't have any change," Kalani said.

"That's okay. Keep the change."

With those words the other three DeVille family members gasped.

"Are you out of your mind spending that much on those tickets?" exclaimed Mrs. DeVille.

"Yeah, they're for *Navajos*!" said Tulsa loudly. "And the dinner is out on the Rez. Someone is bound to see us!"

"That's okay," said Melvin in a calm voice. "By the end of next week, we'll be millionaires. And supporting a Navajo cause will make us look good in the eyes of society. We won't have to beg people to attend our New Year's party like we did last year."

"Thank you, Mr. DeVille," said Kalani politely. "You wouldn't happen to know what time it is. We have to be home by 5 o'clock."

"There's a clock right in front of your face," said Akron, pointing to a wall clock hanging over the fireplace in the adjoining living room. "Don't you know how to read a real clock? Or is digital the only kind they use in Texas to teach kids to tell time?"

"I didn't look in the next room," Kalani said. "I was taught not to snoop when I am in other people's homes. And yes, I can read a clock."

"That's a beautiful clock, by the way," Kalani said as he began to steer the conversation to the real reason for his visit. "It looks antique. Did it belong to your uncle, Wyatt Granger?"

"Oh heavens, no!" said Mrs. DeVille sharply. "That's mine and it's modern. It only looks like an antique. I wouldn't have any of Wyatt's junk in this house. Everything he owned was old and out of style. His stuff is nothing but worthless trash, and I moved everything of his to our cabin up at Vallecito Lake. And now that we are inheriting his money, I'm going to sell all his stuff, even that old atomic clock he liked so much."

Kalani silently nodded his head. Then he added

to all four of the DeVille family, "Thank you very much for your generosity. You've been very helpful."

As he led his brother to their bikes parked in the driveway, a smile played on his face.

Chapter 12
Following Clues

"What's the matter, Kalani?" asked Tamala Henderson that night at dinner. "You're not yourself at all. You haven't touched your food. Your brother is ahead of you; he's on his fourth taco."

Kalani shook his head as if waking from a daydream. "Sorry, my mind was on something else."

"You've been distracted all evening. What's going on?"

"We went to visit the DeVilles today," said Tristen in the silence that followed their mom's unanswered question. "He's been real quiet ever since we left their house. I couldn't even get him stirred up when I started teasing him. I told him basketball was for girls and wrestling's for men."

Kalani just sat there at the dinner table staring at the uneaten taco on his plate.

"You've been working too hard trying to find another will," said the boys' father. "I think you should take a break from your investigation and relax a bit, get your mind off the case and hit it again later. You'll think clearer with a rested mind, see clues you've overlooked before. It helps me when I'm trying to solve a case."

Kalani sat in silence for a moment then seemed to get an idea. "Yeah, maybe I do need a break from all this. Is it okay with you and Mom if Tristen and I go with Danner to Vallecito Lake in Colorado? His aunt has a small cabin there, and he wants to take us to see the mountains around it. He could drive since he's already got his license. And I'd love some relief from this heat down here in the desert. It's cooler up in the mountains."

Mason looked over at his wife who silently nodded her head.

"Okay," he said, "I'm fine with a weekend trip with Danner. Just be sure to take your cell phone in case something unexpected happens."

Kalani sat back with a smile on his face. Then he reached for the uneaten taco on his plate and devoured it in two bites.

∽

Early the next morning, Kalani poked his head into his brother's bedroom. "Hey, get up. I want to get an early start for Vallecito."

Tristen mumbled something incoherent and rolled over on his side, away from the door.

"Okay, you asked for it," Kalani said under his breath, and he tiptoed into the room. He grinned as he carried the mug with the cold marbles over to the bed.

"Some people just never learn," he said to himself as he quickly lifted the covers and tossed the marbles into bed with his brother.

"YOW!" his brother shrieked, rolling away then jumping out of bed. "Okay, okay; I'm up."

"Here, you know the drill," said Kalani handing his brother the empty mug. "Marbles in the mug; mug in the freezer."

"And hurry up," he added as he paused at the bedroom door. "Danner is on his way over right now. You won't have time for breakfast if you dawdle."

ᗰ

"Let's stop by Josh and Dillon's place on the way to Colorado," said Kalani. "I want to tell them what we've found out so far about Wyatt Granger's will."

He was seated in the Rez Rocket on the passenger side of an old-fashioned bench style seat. His brother sat between him and Danner who was driving. "The lane leading to their house is just up the road a bit."

Danner silently nodded his head.

Pulling up to the Gunderson's home, the boys saw a San Juan County sheriff's SUV in front of the dilapidated barn. They watched as a deputy Kalani knew who worked with his father got into his cruiser and drove past them back to the highway. Kalani was out of the Rez Rocket even before the pickup had come to a complete stop. He ran up to Josh and Dillon standing in front of the open barn. The look on the Gunderson brothers' faces told him something terrible had happened.

"What's going on?" he asked. "What was Deputy Foutz doing here?"

"We were robbed last night," said Dillon quietly.

"What did they get?" asked Kalani as Danner and Tristen ran up. The Rez Rocket was stopped in front of the barn, its motor still running, both doors wide open.

"All our hand tools," said Josh. "There is no way to lock up this old barn, so it was easy to get into it. Now, we've got no equipment to work on motorcycles with. And I don't know where I'll get the money to buy more."

"Maybe my dad can loan you what you need," said Tristen. "You can pay him back when you get more work."

"Or pay him back by working on our motorcycles for free," said Kalani. "Neither of us are good mechanics."

Dillon looked relieved at the offer, but Josh's face was still sad and stunned.

"I may have some good news for you anyway," said Kalani. He quickly told the Gunderson brothers what he had learned from talking to Riley and Kilian. But he didn't mention the one lead he had gleaned from talking with the DeVilles. If it didn't pan out, Kalani didn't want the brothers' hopes raised only to be dashed later.

When he finished, Dillon's face lit up, but Josh merely turned away and headed for the house, his shoulders slumped as if he carried the weight of the world on them. Kalani silently vowed to find Wyatt's missing will for the Gunderson brothers.

5

"Tourists from the flatlands always ride their brakes down hills like this," Danner said as he downshifted the Rez Rocket into second gear. "They're not used to driving in the mountains. And they don't know to use the engine rather than their brakes to slow their cars when going down a steep hill. I can usually smell their brakes overheating when I pass them going the other way."

"Well, I can smell something overheating in your truck," said Tristen. "Hope it's not *your* brakes."

"Can't be," Danner replied. "I've hardly used them

at all on this hill. It must be my engine overheating; I have a tiny leak in the radiator hose."

They reached the bottom of the hill, and Danner pulled over to the shoulder of the highway. He got out, opened the hood, and saw steam escaping from a hose in the engine. As Kalani and Tristen got out to join him, Danner gently removed the radiator cap, using a rag to grab the hot metal. When the steam cleared from the radiator, he saw that it was as he feared, almost empty. "We can't go on with the radiator this low. I'll have to get some water from a gas station in Durango. You two wait here with the truck, and I'll hike into town."

"I've got some bottled water in my backpack," said Kalani. "I always carry several bottles with me. It's too easy to get dehydrated up in the mountains. And if you do, you'll get altitude sickness."

"There's a disease called altitude sickness?" asked Tristen.

"Yeah, it's what happens when you're not used to being at a high elevation, like in the mountains," his brother answered. "You usually get a headache and are always out of breath. Tourists from sea level often get it. And remember we used to live in Houston, which is right by the ocean, down at sea level."

"Yeah, but you've been here for almost half a year," said Danner, "so you're used to the higher altitude of New Mexico. Flora Vista is almost as high as Durango. If you don't get out of breath playing basketball, then you're not going to get altitude sickness by going to Colorado."

"Well, it's still a good idea to carry water when you travel. You never know when you'll need it."

"Yeah, you're right," said Danner. "I'm glad you thought to bring some. Let me have a bottle so we can get the Rez Rocket fired up again."

The rest of the trip to Vallecito Lake took the boys through the soaring mountains of southwest Colorado. The Henderson brothers were awestruck by the rugged beauty of steep, pine covered peaks with patches of crusty snow peeking out of dark, sunless crags. Having grown up in the swampy flatlands around Houston, they were overwhelmed by the stunning view of mountain summits ranged one behind another. Not once did Kalani's mind dwell on the problem of finding the missing will of Wyatt Granger.

ꙅ

"Well, here it is," said Danner pulling up to a small cabin within sight of the shoreline of Vallecito Lake. "It's pretty simple inside, but I love coming up here. I enjoy the quiet and being close to nature. I guess it's a *Dineh* thing."

"No, it's not just a *Dineh* thing," said Kalani. "I enjoy getting out in nature as well."

"Let's unpack the truck and fix some lunch. Then I'll show you around the lake. My auntie has a small motorboat down by the dock. Let's hope it's working."

After a quick lunch of sandwiches, Danner led the Henderson brothers down to a boathouse on the water's edge. Inside were several empty slips where small boats could be tied up. "I guess people put their boats in here to protect them from bad weather, huh?" said Tristen.

"Yeah, the lake often freezes over during winter," said Danner. "But in here there are ropes and pulleys to hoist the boats out of the water and keep the ice from crushing them. That's generally my chore during the fall: winterizing the cabin and getting my aunt's boat out of the water."

Danner led the boys over to the only slip that had a small boat hanging from the rafters. "Looks like no one's had the boat out this summer yet. It may take me a while to get it running."

Danner's words proved prophetic. It took a couple of hours of work on the motor to get it to crank and run. But after cleaning the spark plug, and replacing the oil, the motor sputtered to life. "Go back to the cabin and get the life jackets while I take the boat over to the marina and get some fresh gas," said Danner to Kalani and Tristen. "The gas in the tank has been there all winter and is probably diluted with water. And bring the binoculars. I want to show you some of the fancy cabins the rich *bilaganas* have built here on Vallecito."

5

"Whoa! Look at that one," said Tristen. "That looks more like a palace than a mountain cabin. Wonder who owns it?"

"That belongs to a rich Hollywood actor and his wife," said Danner. "They only come here a couple of times each summer, and then only if he's not filming a movie."

The three boys were in the small fishing boat of Danner's aunt, slowly cruising the shoreline of Vallecito Lake. Danner was in the rear of the boat, steering the outboard motor and pointing out the palatial cabins owned by the rich and famous. The Henderson brothers took turns looking at the mountain retreats through binoculars.

"What about that one?" said Kalani pointing to another huge cabin a few minutes later while peering through the binocs. "All the windows are boarded up. It looks like no one has been there all year."

"That belongs to a wealthy doctor from California," said Danner. "It's pretty tragic, what happened to him."

Kalani passed the glasses to his brother and

looked over at his Navajo friend for him to continue his explanation.

"He had a ten-year old son who drowned in the lake last summer. He got caught in a sudden thunderstorm while in a small fishing boat, kinda like this one. The wind whipped up some really big waves which capsized the boat, and the kid drowned."

"He wasn't wearing a life jacket?" Kalani asked.

"No, he wasn't. Guess he thought he didn't need one. Or that he'd have plenty of time to see a storm approaching. He didn't know how quickly thunderstorms build up over the mountains and produce a lot of wind and rain. Or how often it happens. Usually every afternoon in the summer."

"He didn't swim to shore when his boat sank?" asked Tristen. "I could swim to shore even from the middle of this lake. Vallecito isn't very wide; just really long."

"No, this water is ice cold, even in summer," said Danner. "It's not like the lakes you grew up around in Texas. Vallecito is fed by runoff from the mountains. Last week this water was snow on the higher peaks and is still freezing cold. And really icy water is harder to swim in because your muscles want to cramp up."

"I'm glad you made us put life jackets on," said Kalani giving the straps on his jacket a tug to tighten them around his body. "I certainly don't want to try my luck swimming in this lake."

∽

After an afternoon of slowly cruising along the shoreline of Vallecito looking at lakeside cabins, Kalani turned to Danner sitting in the stern and asked, "Don't the DeVilles have a cabin up here, too?"

"Yeah they do," said Danner. "It's a little farther down the lake, almost directly across from my auntie's cabin. It will be coming into view in a few minutes."

Within a short time Kalani saw Danner's answer to his question. "Look over there between those two towering Ponderosa Pines and you'll see the DeVille's cabin," his Navajo classmate told him.

Kalani took the binoculars from Tristen and studied the cabin for several minutes. "It looks run down," he said, handing the field glasses back to his brother.

"It is," Danner answered. "The DeVilles seldom spend any time up here. They prefer to stay in Farmington and hob-nob with the rich people there."

"But don't a lot of rich folks have cabins here at Vallecito Lake," asked Kalani. "It seems that this would be the place to party with the wealthy."

"Yes, you're right," said Danner. "A lot of the elite from New Mexico come here to socialize and get away from the heat of the desert. But the DeVille cabin is pretty run-down, and I guess Melvin doesn't want anyone seeing the inside of it."

"Then why buy a cabin up here in the first place?"

"My aunt told me he bought this cabin many years ago after the Missionary Ridge fire destroyed most of the forest around this lake. The area was really ugly with all the burnt trees, and so the cabins around here lost a lot of their value. That's when Melvin bought his. Also, when my auntie bought hers. Over the years, the forest has recovered; the area is beautiful again, and property values have gone back up."

"Why doesn't Melvin fix his cabin up so he can throw big parties for rich folks?" asked Tristen who had been following the conversation.

"He probably couldn't afford to," said Danner. "It's expensive to have someone come all the way out here from Durango to do renovations."

"He'll be able to afford it now," said Kalani. "We heard him say he was getting Wyatt's fortune the end of next week."

Unless I can find a second will, Kalani added to himself. He let out a deep sigh.

"Well, it's getting late," said Danner. "We should head back to our cabin now. It's not a good idea to be on the lake at night with no lights on your boat. It gets really dark up here in the mountains."

Turning the handle of the outboard motor, Danner headed the boat away from the DeVille cabin. Kalani picked up the binoculars and took one last, long look at the cabin, carefully memorizing its location on the lake as the three headed toward the opposite shore and Danner's aunt's cabin.

Chapter 13
Dead End on the Lake

Early the next morning, Kalani poked his head into the bedroom he had shared with his brother. "Hey, get up. Danner wants to go on a hike."

Tristen mumbled something incoherently about Kalani taking a hike—a long one, off a short pier—and rolled over on his side, away from the door.

"Okay, you asked for it," Kalani said under his breath as he tiptoed into the room. He grinned as he looked down at what he carried in a Styrofoam cup: a garter snake that he had found outside the back door. It had been sunning itself, trying to warm up after a chilly night in the mountains. It was still cold in the cup in his hand.

Kalani quickly lifted the covers off his brother and threw the snake against his exposed back then dropped the covers back down. Tristen shrieked and rolled away from the cold object against him. But the snake followed him to snuggle up against his warm body. Tristen shrieked again as he realized that the cold thing in bed with him was alive, and he leaped out of bed.

"Okay! Okay! I'm up!" he snapped as he shivered. He could still feel clammy coldness along his back.

"Come on. Danner wants to go hiking up in the mountains overlooking Vallecito Lake," said Kalani. "And don't forget to put the snake back outside. It's harmless."

∽

Leaning against the counter in the kitchen, Kalani looked up from his plate of scrambled eggs and bacon as his brother stumbled out of the bedroom. He silently shook his head as he watched him walk over with the Styrofoam cup to the kitchen door and toss the snake into the back yard. *Yep, he's definitely not a morning person.*

Kalani poured a mug of coffee for his brother and handed it to him. Tristen leaned against the counter across from him and took a sip.

"What?" he asked when he looked up and noticed his brother smirking at him.

"You're going to have a rough time when two-a-day practices start in a few weeks," Kalani answered him. "You're gonna have to get used to getting up at five o'clock if you want to make the football team."

"You better not have gotten me up that early!" Tristen said, looking out the window to see if the sun was up yet.

"He doesn't like five o'clock," Kalani said to Danner with a laugh. "He just learned last week that it comes twice a day. He thought it was only in the afternoon."

Tristen gave him a dirty look.

Turning back to his brother, Kalani said, "Naw, I wouldn't get you up that early for no reason. It's eight o'clock. But Danner wants to go on a hike, and you need to go with him."

"Why do I need to go with him?"

"In case something happens to him. You should always have a buddy when hiking in the mountains."

"Aren't you going?"

"No, I want to take the boat across the lake and check out the DeVille cabin. That's where Wyatt Granger's belongings are stored. I'm hoping to find his new will there somewhere."

"But wouldn't the DeVilles have found it when they packed up his junk and moved it here from Farmington? He was living with them in their house when he died."

"I'm betting on it being hidden in something," Kalani said. "Remember how Dillon said he once found a lost check in a book because old Wyatt had used it for a bookmark. Maybe his new will is inside a book or a magazine. I doubt if the DeVilles opened all his stuff and looked inside when they boxed up his belongings."

"You want some help looking through his stuff?" asked Danner.

"No, you and Tristen go hiking. I know you're really anxious to get up in the mountains. If I went with you, I wouldn't be able to enjoy anything. My mind would be too focused on where Wyatt could have hidden his will and not on the beauty of the Rockies."

5

Kalani climbed into the small fishing boat tied up at the dock in front of Danner's aunt's little cabin. After it quit rocking, he checked the gas tank on the outboard motor. It was almost empty from yesterday's long tour of the lake and its cabins.

More cautious this time, Kalani climbed out of the small, flat bottomed boat to get a container of gasoline from the boat house. But his inexperience caused him to slosh a little bit of lake water into the boat. It rocked again as he stepped back in. He waited for it to stop before carefully unscrewing the cap of the motor's fuel tank and slowly pouring gas from the can into it. Bent over and concentrating on not spilling anything, Kalani lost his balance for a moment, causing the boat to wobble again. After he caught his balance, he saw the spout of the gas can had come out of the motor's fuel tank and gasoline was spilling into the bottom of the boat. *Be careful, you big dummy,* he thought to himself. *There wasn't much to start with.*

It took several cranks on the rope to start the little outboard motor. Once Kalani had it running, he gently shoved off from the dock and pointed the boat toward where he remembered the DeVille cabin was located.

∽

As he crossed the lake, Kalani heard the motor sputter from time to time. When it did, he felt the boat slow until the motor kicked back up again. About midway across the lake, it quit all together.

Kalani cranked on the starter rope, but the motor wouldn't start. Again, and again he cranked. But it still didn't start. He examined it closely to see if he could see anything out of adjustment, but everything looked like it should. He saw no loose wires or unattached parts.

Again, he cranked on the starter rope, and again it wouldn't start. "I wish Josh or Dillon were here right now. They'd know how to get this thing going," Kalani thought as he stood over the motor and stared at it in frustration.

"Guess I'll call Danner and tell him I'm stuck in the middle of the lake," he said as he pulled his cell phone from his hip pocket. But at that moment a wave hit the boat broadside and caused him to sway and lose his balance. He dropped the phone into the pool of water in the bottom. When he pressed the "home" button to turn it on, nothing happened. He tried again, but the screen didn't light up.

He opened the back of the phone, removed the battery, and replaced it, hoping this would fix the problem. He noticed the inside was wet, and he wiped as much of the moisture out as he could before replacing the battery and closing up the back cover.

He pressed the home button again, but the phone still didn't turn on. He pushed the two volume buttons on the side, but that didn't start it either. With a deep sigh, he realized the water in the boat had probably killed it for good.

Once more, he examined the motor. He unscrewed the spark plug and examined it closely. It didn't appear to be dirty in any way, but then he realized, he probably wouldn't be able to tell if it were fouled or not. Again, he wished one of the Gunderson brothers were with him as he put the spark plug back in the motor.

ᔕ

Kalani sat stranded in the middle of Vallecito
Lake. Every now and again, he would crank on the
little motor, but it stubbornly refused to start. He tried
several times to call his brother or Danner, but he had
no luck getting his phone to work. He was tempted to
throw it into the lake, but he knew that wouldn't help
his situation at all.

Perhaps he could row to shore, so he looked
under the board seats for an oar or something to
paddle with. But there was nothing but ankle-deep
water in the bottom.

For most of the day, Kalani sat in the gently
rocking boat. From time to time he saw fishermen
motor past him in the distance. But every time he
tried to hail them, they simply waved back, thinking
his frantic gestures were merely him waving in
greeting. Each failure to get their help frustrated
Kalani further, and he wanted desperately to whack
the outboard motor. But he knew it would have been
pointless. The motor wasn't his brother he could boss
around. And he would only hurt his hand.

He sighed and let the afternoon sun warm his
back. With nothing to do, he began to think about
Wyatt's belongings at the DeVille's. He hoped they had
moved everything of his up to their cabin. And done
so without examining anything too closely.

As the sun began to sink behind the ridge of
mountains, Kalani gave the starter rope one more
pull. Much to his amazement, the motor coughed

The Mystery of the Lost Will

and sputtered unevenly. He gently fed it a little more gas and the little fishing boat started slowly creeping across the water.

Kalani looked up at the sky and noted dark clouds building over the mountains as they generally did every summer afternoon. He remembered Danner's story about the young kid who was caught in a thunderstorm and had drowned. He sighed; he didn't have enough time to continue across the lake to the DeVille cabin before the wind and rain hit. And he didn't trust the motor to keep running if he did decide to race the storm.

Reluctantly, he turned the boat around and headed back to the dock in front of Danner's aunt's cabin. As he inched slowly across the lake, he wondered, *How am I going to get to the DeVille cabin?*

Chapter 14
Dead End at the Cabin

"Well, didja find it?" asked Tristen excitedly as he placed a large bowl of salad in front of Kalani.

"No, I spent all day in the middle of the lake, broken down," he answered. "And this is what you give me to eat after missing lunch?" His face registered both depression and disgust.

"Hey, it's all I know how to make," his brother responded. "Mom only lets me make salad; guess she thinks I'll learn to like it. But I won't. I didn't fight my way up the food chain just to eat veggies."

"Never mind," said Kalani. "I'll fix myself a sandwich."

Getting up and heading for the kitchen, he continued. "The motor on the boat conked out when I got about halfway across the lake, and I couldn't get it started."

"Why didn't you call someone for help?" Danner asked as he entered the room drying his long, black hair in a thick towel. "We've got good cell phone service up here now. Not like it was a few years back." He had just taken a shower after returning from the long hike with Tristen in the pouring rain and mud. They had been caught in the thunderstorm raging outside.

"I dropped my cell phone in the water in the bottom of the boat. Twice! And there was gasoline mixed in that water, which is probably what did it in."

"I thought the gas went in the motor, not the bottom of the boat," said Tristen with a grin. Kalani shot him a dirty look.

"That little boat wobbles a lot, even if you're being careful with your balance," Kalani continued. "How do you get in and out without slopping water into it?"

"The same way porcupines make love," answered Danner. "Very carefully." He laughed at his own joke.

"Very...Funny," Kalani said, sarcasm dripping from each word.

"Are you giving up your search of the DeVille's cabin then?" asked Tristen.

"No, I'm still determined to find that lost will of Wyatt Granger's."

"You going to try again tomorrow?" said Tristen.

"Yeah, but not in that boat. I don't trust the motor to work tomorrow if it didn't work today. I'm not a good enough mechanic to make it run."

"That's the truth," said Tristen, turning to

Danner. "His mechanical skills are limited to whacking something with a hammer if it doesn't work the first time."

Turning back to his brother Tristen asked, "Well then, how do you plan to get over to the cabin?"

"Guess I'll just have to hike it on foot," Kalani said. "Or maybe catch a ride with someone going over there."

"Be careful doing that," Danner said. "There are some flaky people around here. There's not much of a police presence here. Vallecito is outside the jurisdiction of Durango. And the county sheriff's deputies are spread pretty thin. I've even heard that several cabins were broken into and robbed lately."

"Okay, I'll be careful," Kalani said.

5

The next morning Kalani got up to the smell of coffee and the sound of silence. In the kitchen, next to the coffee pot was a note from Danner. In it he explained he and Tristen were out hiking again, this time early enough to climb up to the top of Miller Mountain before the usual afternoon thunderstorm forced them back down. Kalani wondered what cold object Danner had put in Tristen's bed to get him up so early.

As Kalani leaned against the kitchen counter,

sipping his hot coffee and deciding what to fix for breakfast, he spied the keys to the Rez Rocket hanging on a nail in the wall by the refrigerator. A thought came to him. *I could drive the Rez Rocket to the DeVille cabin, search it, and be back before Danner and Tristen returned from their hike.*

Carefully Kalani weighed the pros and cons of driving the pickup without permission or a driver's license. He was sure that Danner wouldn't mind him borrowing the truck. But on the other hand, his father would be furious with him for driving without an adult, and Kalani couldn't imagine what he would do to him for breaking the law.

Or was it against the law in Colorado to drive a vehicle with just a New Mexico beginner's license? Could he get a ticket in Colorado for breaking a New Mexico law? For that matter, did Colorado even have a beginner's license for teens just learning to drive? And wouldn't any kind of New Mexico license count as his driver's license in another state?

Then another thought came to him. Maybe all this indecision was moot. If he hurried over to the DeVille cabin, searched it quickly, and sped back, he could definitely return the truck before Danner and Tristen got back from their hike.

And even if he didn't beat them back, Danner wouldn't care. And the chances of him being stopped on the road by a cop were small—hadn't Danner mentioned that the sheriff's department was spread thin around the lake? And Vallecito was outside the jurisdiction of the Durango police.

Heck, Kalani thought to himself, *I'll bet I won't even see a cop at all to give me a ticket. And taking the pickup would be safer than trying to cross the lake in an unsafe boat with an unsafe motor. Or trying to hitch-hike and getting picked up by vicious criminals out looking for mountain cabins to break into and rob!*

Yeah, taking Danner's pickup was the only sensible way to get to the DeVille cabin to search it.

With those thoughts, Kalani set his unfinished coffee on the counter, grabbed the keys to the Rez Rocket, and headed for the door.

∽

Once he was sitting in Danner's pickup after starting the motor, Kalani ran into his first problem. The Rez Rocket had a manual transmission. Kalani had never driven a stick shift before, only the automatic transmission of his father's pickup. But Kalani felt confident he could handle it. He had watched Danner drive a lot of times, and his father had explained the difference between the two. How hard could it be?

Clunk! The motor died with a jerk.

Kalani started the engine again, turned to look over his shoulder as he revved the motor up. He let out on the clutch but too quickly, and the Rez Rocket jumped forward like a scalded cat as the engine died once more with another clang.

That was close, you big dummy! Kalani thought to himself. He had forgotten to check which gear the truck was in and had almost run into a tree in front of the pickup. Kalani started the engine again, pushed in on the clutch, and put the truck in reverse, the gears grinding and complaining at his inexperience. Revving the engine until it sounded like the final lap at the Indianapolis Speedway, Kalani gradually let out on the clutch. Very slowly the Rez Rocket began to back out of the driveway and into the dirt road in front of the cabin. Kalani smiled at his success.

After putting the pickup into first gear with more grinding, Kalani frog-hopped the Rez Rocket down the road. He lurched from one side of the road to the other to avoid deep ruts dug by a heavy truck that had driven in the fresh mud from yesterday's rain. Kalani hoped the truck hadn't gone all the way around Vallecito; this was the only road that led to the other side of the lake, and he didn't want to fight the ruts the whole way to the DeVille cabin.

But his luck didn't hold. As he continued along the road around the lake, the deep ruts never turned off on any of the side roads, and Kalani fought the Rocket's steering wheel as he tried to keep his friend's pickup out of them. The road was so rough that he couldn't get going fast enough to shift into second gear. *Well, at least I've got first gear down pat*, he mused to himself.

∽

About an hour later, Kalani saw the DeVille cabin set back from the lake's shore. There was a muddy lane leading up to it from the road, and Kalani saw that the deep ruts he had been fighting all morning continued up to the cabin. "I guess the DeVilles must have torn up this road," he thought to himself. "They probably brought another load of Wyatt's belongings to their cabin last night."

He stopped in the middle of the road immediately before the turn into the long driveway, undecided if he should drive up it or not. He decided not to when he saw there wasn't enough room in front of the cabin to turn around. He didn't want to try to back the Rocket all the way down the driveway after finishing his search for the will. So, he parked Danner's pickup over on the shoulder of the road, got out, and walked up to the DeVille property.

As he approached the building, Kalani could see that the front door was slightly ajar. Thinking this was a little strange, he stopped short, not sure if he should continue up to the cabin or not. He didn't want another run in with the DeVille twins.

Standing at the door, he carefully listened, and

hearing nothing, he knocked. The door creaked open from the pressure of his knock. He peered inside and saw an empty room.

"Hello, anyone home?" he said without raising his voice.

Hearing nothing, he pushed the door open all the way and stepped in. The front room was bare but looking down he could see where a large rug had covered most of the floor. The outline of it was visible in a thin covering of dust. He walked around the clean area where the rug had been and saw small spots in the dust. He bent over and peered closely at them. After a moment, he realized they showed where the legs of chairs and a couch had been.

He looked up and saw on the walls dark rectangles indicating where pictures had once blocked the sun from fading the wallpaper. The whole room had the appearance of having been recently emptied.

He went into the adjacent kitchen. There, he saw all the cabinets and drawers open and empty of plates, cups, pots, and pans.

As he stood motionless in the middle of the room, it dawned on Kalani. Someone had broken into the cabin and robbed it of all its furniture!

Kalani felt his heart drop as he thought about his quest to examine Wyatt Granger's possessions stored somewhere in the cabin. He hurried from the kitchen and searched the other rooms for anything that had once belonged to old Wyatt.

The rest of the cabin was just as bare as the front room and kitchen—all the rooms, that is, except for the second bedroom at the back of the cabin. There, he found it almost empty; all that remained were a large, rolled up rug and a set of bunk beds.

Kalani's shoulders slumped as he realized the worldly goods of Wyatt Granger were missing. And gone too was any chance of finding the second will.

Chapter 15
Encounter with Thieves

As he made his way slowly back to the front door, Kalani thought how this tragic turn of events would devastate Josh and Dillon, Riley and Kaylee. Their disappointment in not inheriting part of Wyatt Granger's fortune was going to be, in large part, his fault. If he had kept his nose out of other people's business, the old man's kind neighbors and relatives would not have had their hopes raised about another will, one that would solve their money problems. Kalani felt horrible knowing he was about to be responsible for letting them down.

Kalani was so absorbed in his failure that he didn't hear a heavy car door slam shut. He arrived at the open front door of the cabin and saw three men who had just climbed out of a blue and black van. As they approached the cabin, he saw that they were not members of the DeVille family!

In an instant Kalani realized these were the men

who had robbed the cabin. And they were coming back to pick up the remaining rug and beds.

Quickly he ran back to the nearest bedroom, but there was no place to hide. He recalled seeing a closet in the farthest bedroom, but that was where the rug and bunk beds were located. The robbers would be headed for that exact room. He heard them enter the house and head his way to finish their burglary. He didn't have time to run and hide in the closet before they would spot him.

Kalani dashed behind the door of the first bedroom, and quietly pulled it all the way open so he was concealed behind it, his back against the wall. He was glad he was thin enough to fit into the cramped space.

He heard the robbers' footsteps just inches from where he hid as they walked heavily past him to the back room. He held his breath, not daring to breathe as they went by. He hoped he wouldn't have to sneeze or cough.

But it was his stomach that gave him away. Just as the last robber was passing his hiding place, his stomach gave a loud growl! He hadn't eaten anything for breakfast, and his belly was telling him about it.

Kalani froze, hoping against hope that the growl hadn't been loud enough to be heard. But the footsteps continued past the door, and Kalani quietly let out his breath. He was safe.

Suddenly, the door he was hiding behind was

shoved all the way to the wall, pinning him and smashing his nose. Then just as suddenly the door swung away from him, and Kalani was staring down the business end of a .38 caliber pistol. He froze instantly, not even daring to wipe the blood slowly dripping down his nose.

"Hey, guys, looks like I found the driver of that old pickup parked on the road," he heard a gruff voice say.

The man motioned Kalani to move away from behind the door as his two companions entered the room. His gun never wavered as Kalani slowly moved to the middle of the empty bedroom. Kalani gently wiped his nose on the sleeve of his tee-shirt, but he never took his eyes off the man confronting him. He realized the thief was very comfortable with guns; he had seen his dad handle his own service revolver just as easily. Kalani was not going to give the man any excuse to shoot him. And both of the other two men had guns tucked into their belts. Escape was out of the question.

"Well, well, what do we have here?" asked one of the two partners of the gunman. He was as tall as Kalani and had a scar that went from the corner of his left eye to the edge of his lip. "Kinda young to be a thief, ain't ya kid?"

Kalani didn't say anything but backed up a few steps as Scarface walked up to him. He wanted to keep

all three men in his sight as they spread out inside
the room.

"This is *our* job," Scarface continued, getting
right in Kalani's face. "Go find your own cabin to loot."
He backed up a little and looked him up and down.
"That is, if you get out of here alive."

Kalani kept his face unmoving, hoping Scarface
wouldn't see the fear he was beginning to feel. A
brief thought passed through his mind that maybe
he could bargain with the robbers, that they wouldn't
shoot him if he promised not to turn them in to the
police. But Kalani realized they wouldn't fall for such
a promise; he wouldn't himself if he were a robber
holding a witness at gunpoint.

Kalani and Scarface faced each other in silence
eye to eye for several moments. Finally, Scarface broke
eye contact with a laugh. "I'll say one thing for ya,
kid; you're one cool dude under pressure." Turning to
the third member of his gang, Scarface said, "Go find
something to tie him up with. We'll leave him here
after we get the rest of the stuff loaded in the van."

�‌ᔐ

Well, look at the mess you've gotten yourself into,
you idiot! Kalani thought to himself as he twisted
his wrists, trying to free his hands from the bonds

binding them behind his back. He was lying on his side on the floor of a dark closet in the back bedroom of the DeVille cabin. His wrists were tied behind his back with zip-ties and his ankles zip-tied as well.

His stomach rumbled again, still complaining about no breakfast. *Thanks a lot, you tattletale! You're the reason I'm in this pickle.* But his stomach only answered him with yet another growl of discontent.

Kalani drew his knees up to his chest and rolled on to them, his forehead pressed against the floor. He raised himself up to a kneeling position but stopped, at a loss. How was he going to go from kneeling to standing with his hands tied behind him and his feet bound together?

He thought for a moment and had an idea. He bent forward while still on his knees until his forehead again touched the floor and moved his bound wrists to the back of his knees. From there he fell to his side, keeping his hands up against his legs. Drawing his knees up as close as possible to his chest, he maneuvered his hands past his feet and got them in front of him.

With his zip-tied hands now in front, he was able to raise himself up into a kneeling position again. He was thankful that he had such skinny, long arms and legs. Tristen would never have been able to get his short arms around his thick, muscular legs.

From kneeling he was able to work his way up to

standing. He hopped over to the closet door and tried the doorknob with his bound hands. It was locked!

With another rumble from his stomach, Kalani slowly banged his head against the door. What else could go wrong?

Chapter 16
Involving the Police

Kalani awoke with a start at the sound of someone calling his name. He was sitting in a dark closet, leaning against the back wall, dejected, and exhausted from yelling for what seemed like hours.

"Hey! I'm in here!" he croaked as he crawled on his hands and knees over to the door and banged on it with his zip-tied fists.

"I found him!" Kalani heard someone shout in a loud voice. It sounded like Danner. "Here, in the back bedroom."

Then in a quieter voice, "That you, Kalani?"

"Yeah, I'm in here," Kalani answered, sitting back on his knees. "That you, Danner?"

Kalani heard the lock click and the closet door open. There stood his *Dineh* friend and younger brother.

"Man, you're a sight for sore eyes!" Kalani

exclaimed. "You got anything sharp to cut these zip-ties?"

"Just my wit," said his Navajo classmate with a grin as his brother shook his head. "And this handy, dandy, Swiss Army Knife I got for Christmas."

Danner pulled out a small pocketknife and cut the zip-ties binding Kalani's wrists. Kal rubbed the numbness out of his hands as Danner bent over and cut the ones binding his ankles.

"How did you get tied up in there?" Tristen asked.

"There were some guys robbing this place. They caught me, tied me up, and locked me in here. They were finishing up their robbery when I got here to search the cabin."

"Good thing they left the key in the lock," said his Navajo friend.

"Why did you let them catch you?" his brother asked. "Didn't you see they were robbing the place when you got here?"

Quickly Kalani explained how the burglars had not been there when he first got to the cabin but had returned after apparently taking a load of furniture somewhere. And how his stomach had given him away as he hid behind the door.

"That's the dumbest thing I've ever heard you do!" Tristen said. "You didn't put up a fight at all when they captured you? I gotta show you how to do my guillotine."

"They had guns!" Kalani answered, irritation in his voice. "I wasn't about to get shot."

About that time his stomach gave a loud grumble. Both Tristen and Danner looked down at it and started laughing.

"It's not funny!" Kalani said. "I'm starving. We gotta get out of here and tell the police about the robbery. And stop somewhere to get me something to eat!"

The three boys left the DeVille cabin and started down the muddy driveway. As they walked, Kalani asked his rescuers, "How did you guys find me? What brought you to the cabin?"

"We came down from the mountain early because it was clouding up to rain and I heard thunder," said Danner. "It's dangerous being up on a mountain when there's thunder and lightning. When we got back to the cabin, I saw that the Rez Rocket was gone. When you weren't inside, I remembered you saying you wanted to check out the DeVille's cabin, and I figured you had borrowed my pickup. We waited for you to get back, but after a couple of hours and you hadn't returned, we hitchhiked over here. We found where you had parked the Rocket by the entrance to the DeVille driveway, so we came up to the cabin looking for you."

"You didn't notice a blue and black van when you got here, did you?"

"No," said Danner, "why do you ask?"

"Because that's what the thieves were driving. I saw them pull up in it when they came back for the rest of the stuff. They weren't around when I first got here."

"Yeah, I can see lots of tracks in the soft mud," said Danner as he looked down at the deep ruts in the mud. "Looks like they made several trips down this lane."

"Whoa! Check out these tracks," said Kalani as he stopped and peered closely at them. "The tires on the van are old and almost bald. See, there's no tread left on any of these tracks."

"Good eyes," said Danner. "I didn't notice that at all."

"Comes from having a great detective for a dad," Kalani answered. "I'll bet we can track the van when it gets back on the road from the lack of tread on its tires."

As the three approached the pickup, Danner asked Kalani, "I hope you have the key on you; I didn't see it in the Rocket when we searched it, looking for you."

Grinning, Kalani dug out the key from his pocket and handed it to Danner. "Glad those crooks didn't frisk me and take your pickup too."

"Me too," answered Danner.

"Now let's get me something to eat and tell the police about the robbery. I'm hungry enough to eat even one of Tristen's salads."

Tristen poked his older brother in the ribs as the three climbed in the Rez Rocket.

5

"Whoa, slow down boys!" said the deputy sitting behind a large desk. "One at a time. I can't understand a thing you're saying if all three of you speak at once."

After stopping at a local McDonald's to get something to go, Kalani, Tristen, and Danner drove into Durango and headed for the Sheriff's office. There, they were ushered to a seated deputy where they began to report the break-in and robbery of the DeVille cabin.

"Now, what's this about a burglary at Vallecito Lake?"

After catching his two friends' eye, Kalani started to recount how he had been captured. Gradually the full story came out with Tristen filling in details about how he and Danner had hitchhiked to the cabin. As the words came tumbling out, the deputy jotted down notes on a pad of paper on his desk.

"Not to call any of you a liar, but I do need to go see for myself that a burglary has taken place," said the deputy, grabbing his hat and checking his gun strapped on his hip. Looking at Kalani he added, "You ride with me and give me directions to the cabin. You other two follow me in your vehicle."

ᔕ

"I'd park down here by the road if I were you," said Kalani as the sheriff's cruiser approached the entrance to the muddy driveway leading to the DeVille cabin. "That way, you won't wipe out the tracks of the van they used to haul off stuff from the cabin."

"Good thinking on your part, kid," said the deputy sheriff.

As Kalani and the deputy walked up the driveway, Tristen and Danner ran to catch up with them.

"Be careful not to step in these tracks," Kalani cautioned his brother. "We can probably learn something about the van that made them after we check out the cabin."

"Yes, your Majesty," said Tristen, sarcasm in his voice. "Anything you say, your Exaltedness."

Kalani shot his brother a dirty look; Danner just shook his head.

"You two argue like this all the time?" asked the deputy.

"Yes," said Danner."

"Only when he bosses me around," said Tristen at the same time. "It's constant."

"Now I understand why the two-hour delay in searching for you," said the deputy more to himself.

5

As they approached the cabin, the deputy held out his arm to stop the three boys before they walked up to the partially opened front door.

"Was the door locked or unlocked when you got here," he asked Kalani. "Was it open or shut?"

"It was a little ajar—not closed tight. It opened a little more when I knocked on it."

Carefully the deputy examined the door and the jamb. "It doesn't look forced. I think someone had a key."

"It may not have been locked at all," said Kalani. "If Akron was the last person to bring stuff here to the cabin, he's dumb enough to have left the front door unlocked."

"You know the owners of this cabin?" asked the deputy.

"Only from school," said Kalani. "We're not exactly good friends."

"Then why were you here looking through their stuff?" the deputy said, looking at Kalani with suspicion.

"I was searching for something that belonged to their great-uncle. He had hidden it before he died. It was his will."

"And did you find it?"

"No, everything was gone when I got here except for a set of beds and a rug."

"So, you didn't take anything at all?" said the deputy looking at Kalani intently.

"No sir," Kalani said seriously. "There was nothing to take. And if there were, I'd need help or something to take it in."

"What about your brother and your friend here? And their pickup?"

Kalani gulped as he realized what the deputy was implying.

"No sir, we didn't take anything at all. The robbers had me tied up in a closet. And Tristen and Danner were hiking in the mountains all morning."

Slowly the deputy looked each boy in the eye. Danner stood there silently, and Tristen went pale.

Returning his gaze to Kalani, he asked, "You're Mason Henderson's son, aren't you?"

"Yes sir, and so is Tristen."

"And you're Mrs. Peter's nephew, aren't you?"

Danner nodded his head silently.

"Well, I'm going to give you three the benefit of the doubt," the deputy said to Kalani. "I know Mason, and I'm sure he's raised honest, upstanding boys." To Danner he added, "Your aunt is very respected around here, and I'm sure she helped raise you to be honest and law-abiding."

Kalani heard his brother let out his breath.

"Thank you, sir," said Kalani.

Turning to the door, the deputy said, "Let's take a look inside." And he gently pushed it open.

Inside, Kalani pointed out the areas of the floor and walls not covered by dust or faded from sunlight, showing where a large rug had lain, and pictures had been hung. In the kitchen, he again showed the open drawers and cabinet doors where the thieves had taken the plates, cups, and silverware.

"And here is the closet where they tied me up and locked me inside," Kalani said as he led the deputy into the back bedroom. Looking inside the closet, the deputy bent over and picked up the two zip-ties that had bound Kalani, still zipped but cut by Danner's knife.

"Well, this agrees with your story," the deputy said as he placed them in a sandwich bag he had taken out of his pocket for evidence.

All three boys let out a sigh of relief.

After a thorough look in each room of the cabin, the deputy led the three outdoors to examine the deep tracks left by the van.

"I noticed there is no tread showing in the tracks," Kalani told the deputy. "I figure the tires must be so old they're bald. It should be easy to follow the van and see where it went after leaving the cabin."

"Until it gets back on pavement," said Tristen, interrupting his brother.

"Did any of you get a look at the van?"

"I did," said Kalani. "It was small, blue and black,

with a picture of a man pushing a dolly with boxes on it. Well, not a picture like a photo, but more like a cartoon."

"That should make it easy to spot on the highway," said the deputy. "I'll get an APB out on it."

"APB?" asked Tristen.

"All Points Bulletin," answered his brother. "It goes out to all the cops in the area to be on the lookout for someone or a certain vehicle. Honestly, sometimes I wonder if you actually listen to anything Pop says. You should know what an APB is from hearing him talk about them all the time."

"Well, exCUSE me, Mr. Know-It-All, but I don't eavesdrop on other people's conversations."

"No, you never pay attention to what's going on around you," said Kalani.

"Okay you two," interrupted the deputy. "Stop the arguing. I'll get the word out to be on the lookout for a blue and black van with artwork of a man pushing a dolly with boxes."

The walk down to the road was made in silence. Once there, the deputy examined the tires of Danner's Rez Rocket. "Nope, these tires are fairly new. This pickup hasn't been up to the cabin at all."

"Hey, check out these tracks," said Tristen. "The van turned right when it got to the road."

"Good job noticing that," said Kalani. "Now we know which way it headed."

Tristen's face lit up with his brother's compliment.

Chapter 17
The Biker's Clue

"Now what do we do?" asked Tristen. "They could have gone left, right or straight ahead."

Tristen was seated between Danner and Kalani in the Rez Rocket which was stopped behind the deputy's cruiser. The two vehicles were located at the four-way intersection of the road from Vallecito Lake and the major highway out of Durango. As the three boys watched, the deputy sheriff got out of his cruiser and walked over to Danner sitting in the driver's seat.

"Any idea which way they went?" Kalani asked the deputy, leaning forward to talk over Tristen and Danner.

"No, but I've got other deputies looking for them on the highway," he replied. "If they turned west, they'll be heading to Durango, and I've got the Durango Police on the lookout for their van. If they turned east, they'll be heading for Pagosa Springs, and there's a sheriff's cruiser patrolling that section of the highway. If they went south, they'll be headed toward the Ute Reservation, and I've got their police on the lookout for them. But since the Utes don't have jurisdiction off their reservation, I'll head that way and search the stretch of road between this intersection and the Rez."

"I noticed a small dirt road heading off to the left a ways back," said Kalani pointing back up the Vallecito road they had just driven. "We could check it out; maybe they went that way."

"I know which one you're talking about," said the deputy. "It's a narrow county road leading to the base of Severn Peak. There's not much on that road except some mountain cabins and an old inn. The cabins aren't vacation homes; they're occupied all year round, and the inn is due to open soon, now that the summer tourist season is about to start. There are no empty buildings up that road to hide stolen loot in."

"Well, it's worth a shot," said Kalani. "We'll let you know if we find anything."

ᔕ

"Pull over for a minute," said Kalani to his Navajo classmate.

Danner shot Kalani a questioning glance as he pulled the Rez Rocket over to the side of the paved road. He was about to turn on to the road leading to Severn Peak.

"I want to check out the county road," Kalani answered his friend's silent question. "It's not paved, and there may be tracks in the dirt showing the robbers went that way."

Danner nodded his head as Kalani jumped out of the pickup. Walking over to where the county dirt road met the paved road leading to Vallecito Lake, Kal carefully searched both. A few minutes later, he returned and climbed back in the cab, a disappointed look on his face.

"Well, what did you find?" asked Tristen after his brother sat there for several moments, saying nothing.

"I couldn't tell if they went up the dirt road or not," Kalani said. "I saw some fresh tracks, but no bald ones made by the van. If the robbers drove up that way, their tracks were wiped out by someone driving over them afterwards."

"You giving up?" asked Tristen.

"Nope, I've got to find Wyatt's stuff and see if there's a will somewhere in it." To his *Dineh* friend he said, "Drive down this county road but go slow. I'll check every little bit for the van's tracks."

Danner nodded silently, slipped the Rez Rocket into first gear, and started down the road. Kalani was impressed with how smoothly he did it.

∞

The next half hour was spent creeping down
the road in first gear. Every dozen yards or so,
Kalani would tell Danner to stop while he got out
and searched the road ahead. But the results were
always the same: any tracks that could have been
made by the van were obliterated by other vehicles
driving on the road later. Kalani was beginning to get
discouraged of ever finding Wyatt's missing furniture.

He was about to give up and tell Danner to turn
around when he saw a cyclist walking her bicycle
toward them. "Pull over and let me ask this girl if
she's seen the van," Kal said to his classmate.

As they came to a stop near the cyclist, Kalani
noticed she looked like she had had a crash on her
bicycle. She had scraps and dirt on her bare legs and
face, her riding shorts and shirt covered in mud.
Both tires were flat, and the chain had come off the
sprocket.

"Are you all right?" Kalani asked as he got out of
the pickup and walked over to her. "What happened?
Did you crash?"

A young girl about Kalani's age nodded her
head. "I got run off the road and into the drainage
ditch. I landed on rocks and scraped my hands and
knees. The crash flattened both tires and bent the
sprocket so much the chain wouldn't stay on."

Kalani noticed she must have also hit her face because there was a cut on her cheek and her bottom lip was swollen.

"You need a ride somewhere?" Kalani asked. "Where are you headed?"

"Yes, I'd love a ride. I'm heading back to Durango to the bike shop where my boyfriend works. I'm hoping he can fix my bike."

Kalani walked back to Danner in the pickup and explained what had happened and his offer to take her back to Durango.

"I've got a first-aid kit behind the seat," Danner said. "Does she need any bandaging?"

"Yeah, I think she does," Kalani said. "And some water to wash off the dirt. You have any left?"

While Danner dug out the first-aide kit and gallon jug of water to tend to her injuries, Kalani walked her bike to the rear of the pickup, lowered the tailgate, and put it in the bed. Her injuries seen to, she climbed into the bed and leaned up against the cab. Kalani jumped in with her.

"You want to sit up front, inside?" Kalani asked her.

"No, I'm fine back here," she said.

"I'll ride back here with you," Kal said, sitting down beside her, his back also against the cab of the pickup.

As Danner turned the Rez Rocket around in the narrow dirt road, Kalani asked her, "Who ran you off the road? And why didn't they stop to see if you were all right?"

"It was a van," she said. "And they kept on driving like they didn't even see me. But I know they *did* because they swerved over to hit me. I heard them drive up behind me, but I thought they would move over to the other side of the road to give me plenty of room since there was no other traffic. But as they got closer, I glanced over my shoulder and saw a man in the passenger side stick his head and shoulder out of the window. As they drove by, he slapped me on the back. The force of his hit knocked me off balance and I landed in the ditch."

"What did this van look like?" Kalani asked.

"It was small, blue, with a man pushing a dolly."

"That's the van we've been looking for!" Kal exclaimed.

"They're friends of yours?" she asked as she drew back from him.

"No, they robbed a cabin on Vallecito Lake, and the cops are looking for them."

After a moment's thought, Kalani asked, "How long ago did this happen? And where along this road?"

"About three hours ago, close to the parking lot of Severn Peak. There's a bike trail going up the mountain from there, and my boyfriend and I plan to ride it tomorrow. I was going out to the base of the mountain to check out how muddy the parking lot is from all the rain lately when those guys in the van ran me off the road."

"Do you know the area along this road very well?"

"Yes, I grew up in Durango, and I ride all the back roads around here."

"What's between where we picked you up and the parking lot?"

"Just a couple of cabins and the Pine Tree Inn," she said. "It's supposed to open next week for the summer tourist trade."

"Any place where someone could store a big load of furniture?"

"Maybe at the Pine Tree Inn, but it's boarded up tight. They'd need a key to get in."

She paused for a moment, thinking. "Well, maybe not. The owners have a crew cleaning up the place after being closed all winter. But more furniture would certainly get in the way of the workers."

Kalani sat back against the cab of the Rez Rocket, his mind racing with possibilities.

Chapter 18
A Dangerous Discovery

"What are we going to do now?" asked Tristen as he ate the last of his hamburger. He was seated with his brother and Danner in a small, local café in Durango. The three had decided to stay in town after dropping off the bike rider at her boyfriend's shop and go somewhere to eat rather than drive all the way back to the cabin to fix something for dinner.

"I want to check out the Pine Tree Inn," said Kalani. "I've got a feeling that's where the thieves took the stuff from the DeVille cabin."

"Wouldn't it be more likely they took it to one of the cabins on that road?" asked Tristen. "Someone on the work crew at the inn is gonna ask questions about a lot of stuff suddenly showing up."

"Not if they thought the owners were replacing the furniture at the inn," said Kalani.

"No, I think Tristen is right," said Danner. "I'll bet someone living in one of the cabins is working with the thieves and letting them store their stolen loot at their cabin."

"Yeah, that's a possibility as well," said Kalani. All three boys sat in thoughtful silence. Kalani weighed the likelihood of each place being the location of the stolen furniture.

Coming out of his contemplation, Kalani looked over at his brother's plate. "Hurry up and eat your fries. I want to check out the Pine Tree Inn before nightfall."

Tristen covered his French fries with ketchup and started eating them with his fingers, ignoring the unused fork by his plate.

ᔕ

"I still think we should scope out the cabins first," said Tristen, seated between his brother and Danner on the bench seat of the Rez Rocket. Danner had pulled his pickup into the parking lot at the foot of Severn Peak so that the three could decide where to search for the stolen furniture from the DeVille cabin. Danner nodded his head in agreement with Tristen's proposal.

"I don't know," said Kalani. "I've got a strong feeling we should check out the inn first. That's where I would take the loot if I had stolen it."

"But that's in plain sight," said Tristen. "Too many

people would see furniture being unloaded and ask questions."

"That's the best place to hide something—in plain sight," said Kalani. "And if anyone did see another load of furniture, everyone would think the owners were redecorating."

"Well, at a cabin, not as many people would know about the stolen stuff. And if the owners of the cabin were working with the thieves, they wouldn't say anything to anyone about the loot."

"Why don't we do both?" said Danner, interrupting the two brothers. "As late as it is, it'll be too dark soon to look for truck tracks in both places unless we split up."

"Good idea," said Kalani.

Danner fired up the Rez Rocket and pulled back on to the road. Driving for several minutes, he stopped in front of a large, flowery sign labeled *The Pine Tree Inn*. A narrow lane covered in dried pine needles led through a dense forest of Ponderosa and Lodge Pole Pines to a large, two-story building in the distance.

"I'll go check out the inn. You two go back and check out those cabins we passed on the way," said Kalani as he stepped out of the pickup. "Meet me back here at this spot when it's too dark to look for tracks any more. Tristen, loan me your cell phone. Mine's trashed from being dropped in the water. Danner's got his if you two need to contact me."

Danner nodded silently as he started up the Rez Rocket and headed back up the road.

∽

Kalani slowly searched the narrow lane leading up to the inn for truck tracks but he couldn't see anything. What little late afternoon light there was couldn't find its way through the thick forest, and the dense layer of pine needles from the towering trees was too soft to hold an impression for more than a moment. There was no way to tell if there had been any traffic leading to the inn, let alone a van with bald tires.

He walked slowly up the lane and approached the large hotel. It was quiet, shadowy, its windows unlit—an ominous hulk of a building. To the left of the inn itself, there was a barn, equally big and menacing. And on the inn's right, a large dirt lot where patrons could park their vehicles.

After a moment of indecision, he walked over to the parking lot and saw that it was empty—no van. He looked carefully in the dirt around his feet, but the evening darkness prevented him from seeing tracks of any kind.

Kalani turned and mounted the large veranda that spanned the entire front of the inn, heading for the barn on the other side of the hotel. As he passed one of the front windows, he saw a light peeking through heavy curtains and heard loud laughter. He stopped in front of the window and listened.

"Here, hold my beer and watch this," he heard a man's voice say. There was silence for a moment, then a loud crash and a moan followed by more laughter. Someone had fallen on a piece of heavy furniture and broken it. A voice said over the laughter and groaning, "Ed, you're dumber than a box of rocks!"

Kalani recognized the voice of the person mocking Ed. It was Scarface, the thief he had had the stare-down with in the DeVille cabin. Kalani had found the three thieves!

Now, to find where they had stashed the stolen furniture of Wyatt Granger and its hidden will.

∽

Kalani tiptoed softly across the large, front porch of the inn and quietly vaulted over the low railing at the far end, landing silently on soft pine needles. He hurried to the barn and looked over its huge, front, double doors. He noticed they were wide enough to drive a large truck though. A closer look showed him they were locked with a new padlock. Tugging on it, the lock didn't budge, and he cringed at the loud thump it made when he let go of it.

Kalani wasn't about to give up so easily, and he

went around to the back of the barn. There, in the growing darkness of twilight, he found another door, normal sized, with no lock on it. He tried to open it and discovered he could turn the handle. But the door wouldn't open when he pushed. Giving it a heavy bump with his shoulder, he heard a clatter from the inside as something fell.

He cautiously opened the door wider, not sure of what was behind it. The hinges screeched loudly, causing him to grimace at the clamor. He paused, listened carefully, and entered the darkness. He immediately stepped on something on the floor and made a loud racket. He froze at the noise then took out Tristen's cell phone and turned on the flashlight app. He looked down at his feet and saw a snow shovel. It had been propped against the door and fallen when he shouldered it open.

Slowly, he moved the light around the interior. In front of him was a small, open space surrounded by a wall of hay bales stacked higher than his head. A narrow walkway between the bales led to front part of the barn.

He walked slowly through the gap in the hay and entered the main area of the building. There, parked inside, sat a small, blue and black van with a cartoon of a man pushing a dolly with boxes on it. And lying haphazardly all over the inside the barn were piles of old, used furniture. Kalani smiled as he realized he had found the missing contents of the DeVille cabin at last.

5

With Tristen's cell phone in his hand, Kalani started to text Danner. He needed his classmate and his brother to come help search Wyatt's possessions for the missing will. But on the cell's face were the words NO SERVICE. Kalani would have to find it on his own.

He started examining the furnishings of the cabin using the flashlight app on the phone, looking for anything that might contain the will. The stolen furniture was lying in a chaotic manner around the walls of the barn and in no noticeable order. Kalani sighed and wished Tristen and Danner were there to help.

Some of the chests and large boxes contained books and magazines, and he thumbed through them looking for a folded piece of paper. Other boxes contained clothes, and he rifled their pockets for a wallet or a loose sheet of paper.

After searching everything on one side of the barn and finding nothing that might contain a will, Kalani went over to the other side where the rest of the furniture was located. Again, he picked up and examined everything small enough to lift and opened anything bigger to search inside.

Finally, after moving the headboard of a large, queen-sized bed, he saw in the light of the cell phone the back side of a circular object. It had a small hook for hanging on a wall. Kalani picked it up and turned it over. He grinned as he looked at an older version of the atomic clock hanging on the wall in Kilian and Kaylee's kitchen. But just at that moment, he heard loud, drunken voices and the sound of someone fumbling to unlock the large padlock on the front doors.

Kalani was about to be discovered by the thieves. Again!

Chapter 19
A Narrow Escape

Thinking quickly, Kalani turned off the cell
phone and fled for the narrow gap in the hay. As
quietly as he could, he slipped into in the small,
open space in the back of the barn and stopped. He
remembered the fallen snow shovel somewhere in
front of the rear door but wasn't sure exactly where
it lay. Evening's twilight had fallen into night's full
darkness, and Kalani could barely make out the
outline of the open door, let alone anything lying on
the floor in front of it. He couldn't see where the snow
shovel lay, and he didn't want to step on it again,
make a racket, and alert the thieves to his presence.

And he dared not use the phone's flashlight app
to see his way out since the wall of hay bales didn't
go all the way up to the ceiling. He was sure the
light from the phone would show on the ceiling and
give him away. He decided to wait in the small space

behind the stacks of hay. If he were quiet, the men wouldn't know he was there. Or so he hoped.

As he stood quietly among the hay bales, he realized he still had Wyatt's old clock in his hands. He grinned as he remembered his visit to Kilian and Kaylee's trailer and how their clock had astonished him as it reset itself. Then his face froze in terror as he also remembered how the clock had loudly chimed when it had done so.

He hoped the battery of the clock was dead and the clock wasn't working. But with the luck he had had recently, he feared there would still be enough charge in the battery to run the clock. It would also be just his luck for it to chime while he was hiding and give him away to the thieves. The safe thing to do would be to remove the battery. And do so with no noise.

Kalani felt around the clock, searching in the darkness for the battery. He ran his fingers over the smooth back covering but couldn't find where the battery compartment was located. Nor could he find any kind of latch to open up the inside. All he felt were three finger holes at the four, eight, and twelve o'clock positions of the flat, even, back cover.

He poked his finger in one of the holes and gently tugged. He felt the cover gently yield to his pull and come off in his hand. He put it under one arm as he felt around the inside of the clock for the battery. He found it, took it out, and put it in his jeans pocket. As he took the cover from under his arm to put back on the clock, he felt a small, flat object taped to the inner side. He hurriedly peeled it off and put it in his pocket with the battery.

Just then, he heard loud voices coming from the other side of the wall of hay bales. Someone shouted to someone else "to leave before they got shot!" Kalani remembered he was supposed to meet Tristen and Danner after it got dark, but his long examination of the stolen furnishings had made him lose track of time. He was late for his rendezvous. He guessed his brother and classmate had come up to the inn looking for him. He hoped his brother wasn't foolish enough to try and tackle the bandits himself.

Kalani set the clock and its back cover down at his feet, leaning them carefully against a bale of hay. He walked over to the back door, nervously feeling with each step for the snow shovel lying somewhere on the floor. He found it before tripping and breathed a sigh of relief as he quietly stepped over it. Once outside, he softly closed the door, hoping the noise of the argument would cover up the squeal of the hinges.

He ran around to the front corner of the barn and stopped, hiding in the shadow of the building as he pressed himself against the side wall. From there, he watched the taillights of the Rez Rocket disappear down the dark driveway, heading away from the inn. He dared not yell to Danner driving the pickup lest the thieves hear him. He didn't want a repeat of the DeVille cabin imprisonment.

Kalani peeked around the corner of the building to see if the thieves were still outside, but the area in front was empty, the doors wide open, the barn quiet. He wondered where they were and wished they were still arguing. That way, he would know their exact location, and their noise would mask his footsteps when he fled the barn's cover. But he decided he would have to take his chances in the silence. He just hoped they were so focused on the stolen loot they wouldn't hear him as he made his escape.

Kalani eased away from the barn and headed toward the pine forest a dozen yards away and the county road beyond. He kept the side of the building between him and the front door. He didn't want to be spotted by the thieves should they came outside. He let out a sigh of relief once he was inside the dark, protective shadows of the thick trees.

The woods were pitch black, but Kalani rejected the idea of turning on the cell's flashlight app. He slowly made his way toward the county road, stumbling often on fallen branches invisible in the deep gloom.

Suddenly, he was lit up by a blinding light like an escaped convict caught in the glare of a searchlight. He froze, not daring to breathe. He knew any movement would draw the attention of whoever was shining the brilliant light into the woods. He waited for the inevitable "Hands up, kid!" from Scarface. But just as quickly, the light moved from shining directly on him to shining on the trees in front of him. He heard the roar of a car engine as it drove past him, and he turned to look. In the driveway leading away from the inn, Kalani caught a glimpse of a man with a dolly painted on the side of a black and blue van. The thieves were driving off, and he had not been seen!

Many minutes later, he emerged from the blackness of the forest into the star-lit openness of the dirt road and looked for either the Rez Rocket or the thieves' van. But the road was empty in both directions.

Kalani was undecided about what to do as he stood in the middle of the road. The plan had been for Tristen and Danner to wait for him at the entrance to the lane, but it seemed they had gone to the inn looking for him when he didn't show up. Their sudden appearance at the barn must have frightened the thieves into fleeing without first loading up the van.

As he stood unsure in the road, he was illuminated by lights from a vehicle coming up the road behind him. Not knowing who was approaching, he bolted into the shallow drainage ditch lining the road, ready to flee back into the woods. But he let out a sigh of relief as the Rez Rocket stopped in front of him, and Tristen's smiling face leaned out the window.

"Hey bro, you want a ride?"

Chapter 20
Gunfight with Thieves

"Move the Rocket so the headlights shine on this area," said Kalani to Danner sitting behind the steering wheel. "I want to see which way the thieves went." He walked over to where the lane from the inn met the dirt road. Danner turned his truck to shine where Kalani now stood.

In the light of the pickup's headlights, Kalani searched for bald tire tracks in the dirt. He heard his two friends walk up to him.

"Aren't they still up by the inn?" asked his brother as he and Danner helped Kalani search. "We were just up there, and we saw them in the barn. They even threatened us if we didn't leave right away."

"Yeah, I know. I was inside the barn, hiding," said Kalani. "You two distracted them long enough for me to get away without being seen."

"Glad to have been of service," said Tristen, with

a grin. "Now, why are we looking for the van's tracks in the dark?"

"Because the sun's not out to light up the area," Kalani answered. He didn't see his brother's dirty look in the darkness.

"I saw them leave right after you two did," Kalani continued. "I think your appearance scared them into fleeing without even bothering to load up the van. They passed me while I was in the woods. The trees were too thick for me to see which way they turned once they hit this dirt road. So, I'm looking for fresh tracks."

"Here they are," said Danner, pointing to the dust in the middle of the intersection. "Looks like they turned left and headed back toward Durango and Vallecito Lake."

"Come on," said Kalani, as he headed for Danner's pickup. "We've got to notify the police."

5

"What's the phone number of the sheriff's deputy who went with us to the DeVille cabin," said Kalani. "I told him I'd contact him if we found anything."

"I don't know," said Danner as he drove down the dirt road. "I don't remember what he said when he gave us his number."

"You didn't put it on your contact list, Mr.-O-C-D-for-details?" Tristen asked his brother. "Where's your phone, anyway?"

"It died when I dropped it in the water in the bottom of Danner's aunt's boat. So even if I had with me, I couldn't call him anyway."

"Well, how are you going to notify him?" asked Tristen. "I don't remember his number either."

"Google the number for the Sheriff's Department—the Colorado one, not New Mexico's. I don't want to get Pop riled up. He'll blow his top if he thinks we're chasing dangerous criminals. It'll be better if we can say we helped capture them after they're safely behind bars."

As Danner continued down the county road, Kalani called the sheriff's department and gave a description of the three thieves, the van they were driving, and their last known location. At the intersection of the county dirt road with the paved one leading to Vallecito Lake, Danner stopped his pickup and looked at Kalani. "Which way now?"

"Right leads back to Vallecito, and there is no place for the thieves to hide in that direction."

Danner nodded his head in agreement.

"If we go left, we will eventually hit the road to Durango and Pagosa Springs. That's the way I'd head if I were fleeing the cops. Go left, Danner, and we'll try to overtake the van before it gets to the highway. If we don't, we'll head into Durango and notify the sheriff department about what we've learned. Maybe they can catch them if the entire police force is looking for them."

Danner nodded his head and pulled on to the paved road. Several minutes later he stopped at the intersection of the highway connecting the towns of Durango and Pagosa Springs. Turning to Kalani, he looked at him questioningly. Kalani nodded with his head to the right and Durango.

Danner was in the middle of his turn when a cop car with sirens screaming and lights flashing approached from the opposite road of the intersection. Danner continued his turn then pulled over to the right shoulder of the highway and stopped, a look of panic on his face.

"I don't think you used your signal when you made that turn," said Tristen, sitting between Danner and his brother. "Looks like you're gonna get a ticket anyway. Your grandma's gonna shoot you for sure!"

Danner started reaching for his wallet but stopped as the police cruiser sped by the Rez Rocket. Grinning at Tristen and Kalani, he said, "Not today, boys! Let's follow him and see what's up!"

"No, we've got to notify the Sheriff's Department about those thieves," said Kalani. "Anyway, I'll bet we see the cop in a few minutes on the side of the highway giving a ticket to a speeder."

Several minutes later, it looked like Kalani's prediction had come true. They crested a small hill and saw flashing lights in the distance. Two police cars were blocking the highway in both directions. In the grassy median between the lanes sat a lone vehicle, its headlights shining straight at the oncoming Rez Rocket.

Kalani stared at the scene in disbelief. In the headlights of the police cars he saw painted on the side of a van a cartoon of a man pushing a dolly against a black and blue background. The police had cornered the thieves.

At that point Kalani heard the sounds of gunfire.

ⵉ

Kalani was out of the Rez Rocket before it had come to a complete stop. He ran toward the cop's car parked across the double lane highway, its headlights shining on the van in the middle of the median. A Sheriff's Deputy, crouched down behind the cruiser's trunk, looked over at him before he got close.

"Get back in your truck, kid," he yelled. "We've got armed men pinned down, and you could get hit by a stray bullet."

"Those are the men we were trying to find," said Kalani, ignoring the order to stay back and running up to the cop. It was the deputy who had investigated the DeVille cabin robbery with him. "We were on our way to tell you where they were holed up."

At that moment more shots rang out. Kalani ducked behind the cruiser's trunk.

"You stay right here behind my vehicle, out of sight, kid," said the cop. "I've got to go help the other deputy. He's by himself over there and taking shots. I'm his only backup."

"There's three of them," said Kalani. "Anybody else coming to help you two out?"

"Not sure, and don't have time to chat about it. Stay here and out of sight."

The deputy hugged the passenger side of his patrol car and snuck towards the thieves' van located a distance away in the wide, grassy median. Kalani heard no more shots, so he gingerly peeked around the bulk of the police cruiser and peered into the black night.

He didn't see either the cop or any of the thieves in the blackness lit only by the headlights of the two cruisers. It was eerily quiet and dark with no traffic on the highway. Kalani felt rather than saw Tristen and Danner come up and crouch down beside him.

"We heard gun shots," said Tristen in Kalani's ear. "Anyone shot?"

"I don't know. I can't see anyone. I think the thieves are holed up inside the van and the cops are hiding in the tall, overgrown grass in the median."

About that time, the boys heard the sound of the van's engine start up. In a flash Kalani realized the thieves were attempting to drive off. The two cops

were too far from their patrol cars to get back in time
to block their escape.

Kalani was undecided whether he should jump
in the police cruiser and drive it in front of the van
to block it. He had just decided to go for it when he
heard more shots being fired. He looked at the van
and saw its tires go flat as the cops shot them out. The
van stopped, and the driver's and the rear doors were
flung open.

More shots were fired, and Kalani ducked behind
the back of the vehicle again. When the shots stopped,
he moved up the passenger side and peaked over the
hood. He watched as the thieves bolted from the van
in separate directions, and the cops shouted, "STOP!
POLICE! PUT YOUR HANDS IN THE AIR!"

The robbers split up in different directions,
but there were only two officers to pursue three
lawbreakers. The lone robber not being chased ran
toward the parked cruiser where the three teens were
crouched, all hiding by the passenger door. Kalani
said in a stage whisper, "One of them is heading this
way! Get ready to jump him! He's planning to steal
this car and get away!"

A moment later Kalani heard the thief's running
footsteps stop at the patrol car. As he fumbled to open
the driver's door, Kalani ran around the front end.
The man was halfway inside when Kalani got to him.
Without thinking, he slammed the open door on the

man's left leg still outside the vehicle. The criminal screamed in pain.

Kalani saw his brother run around the rear of the car and yank the thief out of the cruiser. He collapsed; his battered leg unable to support his weight. Tristen immediately jumped on top of him and moved his hands and legs into position to put the man in a guillotine. Between his skill as a wrestler and the crushing blow from the car door, the much larger thief was quickly wrapped up in a painful, tortuous tangle of arms and legs, unable to move.

Kalani reached down to the immobilized man and took the gun from his belt. The two brothers grinned at each other, one from the ground, the other standing over him, the gun in Kalani's hand pointed at the thief, the way his dad had taught him.

Chapter 21
What the Clock Was Hiding

"Okay, kid, you can hand me the gun now."

Kalani slowly turned to the speaker behind him, the gun pointed safely down toward the ground. He handed it to the officer hilt first after carefully putting the safety on in full view of the cop. It was the sheriff's deputy who had gone with him to investigate the DeVille cabin burglary, and Kal grinned when he saw who it was.

Kalani pointed to the man on the ground, still in the clutches of his brother's guillotine. "I don't think he's going to run off anywhere. I slammed the car door pretty hard on his leg. I think I broke it."

The deputy looked down at Tristen, then over to Danner standing above the pair on the ground, then back to Kalani. "You three certainly get around a lot. How did you find these criminals?" he asked as he unwound the thief from Tristen's python-like entanglement.

"After we left you this afternoon, we went to check out that dirt road on the way to Severn Peak," Kalani said. "I went up alone to the Pine Tree Inn, and Tristen and Danner investigated some of the cabins along the road. I found the robbers' van and all the stuff from the DeVille cabin inside the barn at the inn."

The deputy had the thief up, handcuffed, and leaning against the car on just one leg since his other one was badly injured. It was Scarface, and he looked at Kalani closely when he heard his story. "You're the kid we found in the cabin and locked in the closet, ain't ya?"

Kalani just grinned at him.

$$\omega$$

"Are you badly hurt?" Kalani asked the sheriff's deputy as he leaned heavily against the police car, the light from the headlights showing his blood-soaked leg.

"Yeah, I think I am a bit," he replied, a grimace on his face from the pain. "But not as bad as this guy." He nodded to Scarface who had collapsed back to the ground.

"Are you in good enough shape to drive him to the hospital in Durango?" Kalani asked the cop with concern.

"I don't know. I thought I was. That is, until I ran over here. I guess the adrenalin hid how serious my wound really is." He paused with a grimace as another spasm of pain wracked his body. Kalani looked down and saw that the blood on the officer's trouser leg was spreading, the flashing red of the police lights making it look gruesome. Kalani hoped it wasn't as bad as it looked.

Kalani turned around, searching for the other police cruiser on the opposite side of the median. He saw its taillights driving off, heading for Durango. Kalani looked back at the deputy. "You need to see a doctor too."

"Are you old enough to drive?" the deputy asked Kalani.

Kalani nodded. "I've got my learner's permit and have been practicing with my Pop. I can get you and this guy to the hospital much faster than an ambulance can get out here," he said. He pointed to the thief on the ground. Like the deputy, his face showed that he was in a lot of pain.

Under the direction of the deputy, Tristen and Danner manhandled the injured thief into the back seat of the police cruiser. As they seat-belted him in, Kalani helped the deputy get into the passenger side of the front seat and made him as comfortable as possible. Kalani got behind the steering wheel, looked around, and gave a sigh of relief. The cruiser had an automatic transmission, not a stick shift like the Rez Rocket. This was going to be cake!

$$\infty$$

It was well after midnight when Danner, Kalani, and Tristen pulled up to their cabin on Vallecito Lake. But the three boys were far too excited to go to bed. They kept recounting the electrifying events of the day to each other, reliving their heroic efforts that led to the capture of the thieves. The officers in the Sherriff's Department had fed their feeling of bravery by praising them for their actions after the robbers had been booked into jail. There had even been a hint at a reward, but Kalani said that wasn't necessary. Capturing lawbreakers was reward enough. His brother poked him in the ribs for saying that.

$$\infty$$

The next morning Kalani was putting on his clothes when he felt something in the front pocket of his jeans. He reached in and pulled out a double-A battery and a small, flat key. *Now, where did you two come from?* he said to himself.

He thought for several moments, going over the events of the day before. With a start, he remembered silencing Wyatt Granger's old clock. He recalled feeling something taped to the inside of the back cover after he removed the battery. It had been too dark to see what it was, and Kalani had absentmindedly stuffed it into his jeans. Now, in the full light of day, he saw that it was a key, one he didn't recognize.

Kalani looked at it closely. Why was there a key hidden inside Wyatt's clock? It wasn't a house key or a car key. It didn't resemble the type of key he used on the padlock for his school locker. And he puzzled at the letters *S. W. B.* etched on it.

Kalani wandered slowly into the kitchen to start the coffee pot. His brother and Danner were both still in bed, and he knew they would both like to wake up to a fresh cup of "java" as his dad called it. As he went through the motions of preparing the coffee maker, his mind kept going back to the key.

He wondered if it belonged to Wyatt Granger. Yet the initials on it didn't match his name. But if it did belong to Wyatt, was it the key to some kind of box still among his possessions in the barn? And what would be so important in the box to cause him to hide its key inside his clock?

The smell of brewing coffee woke Danner up who came into the kitchen and poured himself a cup.

"Do you know what kind of key this is?" asked Kalani, pulling it out of his pocket and handing it to his friend.

Danner looked at it carefully, turning it over and over in his hand. He handed it back to Kalani, "No, I've never seen anything like it before. Where did you get it anyway?"

"I found it among Wyatt's stuff in the barn. I think it's to some kind of box or chest that locks. I'm hoping that's where Wyatt hid his second will. I want to head back to the Pine Tree Inn and search the barn for whatever this key unlocks. Let's find something cold to get Tristen out of bed with."

5

An hour later the Rez Rocket was stopped in front of the Pine Tree Inn, and the three boys just sat there, inside the cab, disbelief on their faces. A sheriff's cruiser blocked the entrance to the barn. They watched in silence as the possessions of Wyatt Granger were loaded into a large police van parked inside.

Kalani slowly got out of the pickup and walked over to the deputy standing by the open barn door. He didn't recognize him.

"Excuse me, sir," he said, "what's happening to Wyatt Granger's stuff?"

The deputy turned to him. "It's being taken into custody as evidence. How did you know this belonged to Mr. Granger?"

"I was the one who discovered it was stolen and hidden here. I notified officer Raybon when we found the thieves."

"Good work, kid. Your parents will be proud of you. Clay mentioned you in his case report."

"Is there any way I can take a look at Wyatt's stuff before it's hauled off?" Kalani asked. "I'm looking for a lost will."

"Sorry, kid, but this needs to be inventoried and held as evidence. It would take a court order to allow you to search it."

"I think the will is in a locked box. Could I at least look to see if there is a box that might have it inside? I wouldn't be taking anything away."

"No, no one is allowed near this stuff until a complete record is made of everything in the barn. Afterwards, you might be able to take a peek at the list after it's made public."

"When will that be?"

"It will take a few days to get everything inventoried and the investigation finished. The list will be made public once the case is closed."

Kalani's face fell, and it showed to the deputy.

"Give me your name and phone number, kid?" the deputy said, taking out a small notebook from his shirt pocket. "I'll make a note for someone to notify you when it's available to the public."

The deputy started writing but looked up from

the notebook in surprise when he heard Kalani's name. "You Mason Henderson's son?"

Kalani nodded his head.

"I'll give you a call myself the moment the inventory is done even if the case isn't closed yet. I've met your dad. He's a good man."

Chapter 22
The Key to the Mystery

Kalani was out the door and running across the front lawn to the police SUV even before the engine was killed. He looked at his dad through the open window, excitement on his face.

"Don't worry, son. I'm not going to park in the driveway," Mason Henderson said. "I know you like to shoot hoops with Danner in the evening."

"No, it's not about where you park," Kalani said in a hurry. "I need your help solving the mystery of Wyatt Granger's second will."

"You found a clue to another will?" his dad asked, climbing out of the sheriff department's SUV he used for work. "That's great! But give me a few minutes to get out of this uniform and grab a cold one. I need to relax a bit. It's been a hectic couple of days."

But Kalani could not keep his enthusiasm in check as he started telling his dad about his adventures in Colorado. He followed him through the house to the master bedroom talking a mile a minute. Even when his dad shut the bedroom door in his face, Kalani kept up his rushed narrative through the closed door.

It was when he got to the part of the story where he witnessed the shoot-out from behind the police cruiser that his dad yanked open the door, his tee shirt only half on.

"You were at a gunfight?" Mason asked in a low, cold voice right in Kalani's face. "What were you doing there? You could have been shot, even killed!"

"We were safe behind the police car," Kalani blurted out as fast as he could, backing up, his father advancing on him like a stalking lion on a gazelle.

"Your *brother* was there too?!!"

Kalani could only nod his head as he leaned back, pressed against the back of the couch, his father's face merely inches from his.

"Do you realize how dangerous that was!? What were you *thinking!!?*"

His dad's voice started growing in volume, and Kalani realized the storm of his anger was passing. He knew his father's bark was much worse than his bite. Mason Henderson showed his angriest with a low, cold voice, a fact that often lulled criminals into a false sense of security. The louder the yelling, the less trouble Kalani was in. But he wasn't out of the woods yet. His dad was still in his face.

"But if we hadn't been there, the leader of the

gang would have escaped," Kalani said in a hurry when his dad paused for a breath. "And in a stolen police car, too!"

Mason pulled back a little from his son. Kalani hurriedly continued, still bent backward over the couch. "I slammed the car door on his leg. And Tristen put him in a guillotine. We kept him captured until one of the cops came over to arrest him. I even had to drive them both to the hospital. The officer had been shot in the leg."

Kalani wasn't sure if mentioning a gunshot wound would set off his dad again, but he figured he would read about it anyway. All the cops in the Four Corners area kept up with what was happening through an intranet of department bulletins and emails. Better to be up front with his father now and take whatever punishment he had coming.

∽

Both Kalani and Tristen watched their dad closely as he came out of his bedroom after changing his clothes. He headed for the kitchen and was silent as he took a bottle of beer out of the fridge and gently closed the door.

Kalani tried to gauge his dad's frame of mind. He saw that he was calm and quiet. *Not a good sign*, Kalani thought to himself. *He's still pissed.*

"Sons," Mason said after taking a drink from the bottle, "tell me again what happened at the gunfight. This time, slowly. And in detail."

Carefully, Kalani described how he, Tristen, and Danner had come upon the roadblock and witnessed the gun battle between the sheriff deputies and the thieves. He told how he and his brother had captured the leader of the gang, and how he had had to drive the deputy and the wounded criminal to the hospital. He went into great detail about the praise the deputies had heaped on the three of them for helping catch the crooks. Maybe his father's anger would soften if he heard how other police officers viewed his sons' heroic actions.

"One of the officers even said there might be a reward," Tristen added after Kalani ended his story. "But Kalani said that wasn't necessary. We were just happy the criminals were caught."

Mason stood quiet for several long moments, leaning against the kitchen counter, his beer in his hand, forgotten. Finally, he looked up at his sons and broke his silence.

"I worry about you two all the time," he said in a soft voice. "I worry about your safety. Not because you do foolish things; you're generally pretty level-headed most of the time. But because you are the sons of a cop. And that's the main reason I moved you and your mother out of Houston. I've put too many thugs in jail over the years. Even criminals behind bars have friends who would gladly do my family harm."

He paused, took a deep breath and a sip from his beer before he continued.

"When I heard that you two were at a gunfight, I lost it. To lose one or both of you due to being at the wrong place at the wrong time…" He stopped, unable to go on.

He sat his beer down and grabbed Kalani in a tight bear hug. "Promise me you won't do anything that dangerous again," he whispered in his son's ear. He released his hug and held his oldest child at arm's length, looking him fully in the eye. He held him there until Kalani nodded his head.

"I promise," Kalani murmured.

Turning to Tristen, he grabbed him in a tight hug. "And you, you knuckle-head. Stop doing everything your brother tells you to do. Not all of his ideas are good ones. Use that head of yours for something other than keeping your ears apart."

Tristen was silent, unable to say anything.

"Now, tell me about this clue you found," Mason said, picking up his beer. He turned his back to his sons so they wouldn't see the tears watering his eyes.

The rest of the afternoon was spent trying

to think of what kind of lock the key could be to. And who the initials *S. W. B.* referred to. The dinner conversation was hijacked by how it had been found and how to locate the box it unlocked.

"Tell me again about the time Killian and Kaylee saw the second will," Mason said over his coffee. His chocolate cake only had one bite taken from it.

"It was the day Wyatt died. Kaylee and her husband were shopping in the grocery store when they ran into their uncle Wyatt. He took two hundred-dollar bills out of his wallet and gave it to them for more groceries. His will and another slip of paper fell out. Killian picked them up and handed them back to Wyatt. The will was on a regular sheet of paper, all folded up to fit in his wallet. The other slip was just a small piece of paper with a Navajo word on it. It was small enough that it didn't have to be folded."

"Did Kilian see what was on that small slip of paper?" Mason asked.

"Yeah, he did," said Kalani. "It was *hozhò*. I asked Danner what it meant, and he said it means 'beauty' and describes the *Dineh* word for balance and harmony in your life. He said that when you have *hozhò*, everything is as it should be, and life is beautiful. Without it, your life is in shambles, out of whack, and disordered. I guess Wyatt was trying to bring balance and harmony back into his own life by writing another will, one that would include those who had helped him when he needed it."

Everyone was quiet, deep in thought. But try as they might, no one at the Henderson dinner table could come up with anything more than a guess to what the key unlocked.

"Guess we'll have to get a court order to search Wyatt's belongings," Mason Henderson said, breaking the silence. He looked over at his oldest son, eyeing his unfinished cake. He pushed the small plate over to Kalani who started eating the rest of his dad's dessert.

Chapter 23
The Secret of the Old Clock

"Damon, thank you for seeing us on such short notice," Mason Henderson said, entering the office of his lawyer friend. "You remember Kalani, my oldest son, don't you? And my youngest, Tristen?"

Damon Weems rose from behind his desk, came around it, and shook hands with the three Henderson men. "Oh yes, I remember them. From Dad's Diner a couple of weeks ago."

Damon pointed to three seats in front of his desk, indicating for them to sit. He returned to his large chair behind his desk.

"You hinted you had some vital information regarding a possible second will of Wyatt Granger's and needed a court order to investigate it further," he said, getting right to the point of the meeting.

"Yes," replied Mason. "I think my sons have found the location of another will, and we need your help to get it."

Damon sat back in his chair, hands pressed together, his fingertips lightly tapping his lips. He didn't say anything, waiting for more information from his visitors.

"Kalani wouldn't let go of the idea of there being a second will, so he pursued a line of clues that, quite frankly, amazed me in how twisted and convoluted a trail it turned out to be. I'll let him fill you in on the details."

Mason turned to his son and nodded for him to take over. Kalani leaned forward on the edge of his chair and poured out the story of interviewing the friends and relatives of Wyatt Granger and learning that another will had, indeed, been written but its location was unknown. He explained how the trail then led him to the summer cabin of the DeVilles at Vallecito Lake, the theft of Wyatt's possessions, and their discovery in a barn. He briefly mentioned the encounter with the three burglars and how they were eventually captured. At that point, Damon's eyes went wide and he look over at the boys' dad. Mason merely nodded his head in silent agreement.

Kalani finished by telling how he discovered the key in the old clock and the problem of figuring out what it unlocked. "We need to look through Wyatt Granger's possessions for whatever it opens. And we need a court order to do that. We're hoping you could help us get one."

"Do you have the key with you?" Damon asked.

Kalani nodded his head as he pulled it out of his pocket and handed it to the lawyer, the letters *S. W. B.* face up so the lawyer would notice them right away.

"I know what this is," said Damon taking a quick look at it. "It's a key to a safe deposit box at a local bank. I've got one just like it in my safe here at the office."

"What's a safe deposit box?" asked Tristen.

"Banks have them in their vaults where customers can store valuable possessions like jewelry and important papers in a place that is very difficult to rob and is practically fireproof," replied Damon. "It takes two keys to open them, one that belongs to the customer and the other that belongs to the bank. Wyatt never mentioned to me he had one rented."

∽

An hour later Kalani was standing impatiently in the lobby of Sun West Bank. With him were his brother, his dad, and his dad's lawyer friend. They were clustered around one of the bank officials as he slowly and carefully looked over a court order allowing Damon Weems to search the contents of Safe Deposit Box number 83 for a will and other legal documents.

"This seems to be in order," the bank official said after a lengthy period.

Finally! thought Kalani to himself.

"But let me double check that this box is, indeed, rented to Wyatt Granger."

Kalani fidgeted as he watched the banker walk into his office and pull up information on his computer screen. After what seemed an eternity, he saw him glance down to the court order then back to the screen. Satisfied, he went over to a file cabinet and took out a ring of keys.

"Follow me," the banker said. He led the four into the bank vault. Inside, three of the walls were lined with small rectangles with two keyholes in each one. There was also a small handle in the center of each rectangle, obviously to pull something out. Kalani guessed he was looking at the exposed side of a lot of boxes recessed into the walls. Some of the rectangles were small—about three inches square. Others were much larger, almost a foot across.

The banker led them to one about four inches wide with the number 83 on it. He inserted a key from the ring into one of the two locks on its face and gave it a quarter turn. He looked over at the group standing by him and asked, "Which one of you has the owner's key?"

Kalani handed him the key found inside the old clock of Wyatt Granger. He watched the banker insert it into the second keyhole and give it a quarter turn. The banker pulled out a closed box about two feet long and took it over to a small table next to the vault's exit.

"According to the court order, you may search this box for a will or a Power of Attorney," the banker said. He stood quietly beside the group, watching their every move.

"What's a Power of Attorney?" asked Tristen.

"It gives someone the right to make legal decisions for someone else, even if they're dead. Or it could give someone the power to make financial decisions for them too. In this case, I'm hoping we find one that gives Damon the power to handle Wyatt's finances."

"Even if Wyatt's dead?"

"Even if he's dead," nodded his dad.

Damon open the lid of the safe deposit box and began to search its contents. He took out a small flash drive, looked it over, then put it on the table next to the box. Next, he pulled out several folded sheets of paper stacked neatly under the flash drive. He unfolded each one, looked at it quickly, then refolded it. Finally, he unfolded a sheet of lined paper. Damon read it, smiled, and looked up at Mason Henderson and his two sons.

"Eureka! We have found it!" he exclaimed. He showed everyone a sheet of paper with the words *Last Will and Testament of Wyatt Granger* hand-written across the top.

Kalani glanced quickly at the bottom of the sheet

and saw two signatures. One of them was Wyatt's. And next to the second signature at the bottom, the paper was crinkled where the embossing seal of a notary public had been crimped into it.

$$\infty$$

Back in Damon Weems' law office, Kalani huddled over the shoulder of the lawyer, looking at the screen of a desktop computer. "Try *turquoise*," he said to the lawyer. "That's how he made all his money." Damon typed the suggestion, but the screen blinked in large red letters *INVALID PASSWORD*.

The will of Wyatt Granger found in the safe deposit box had revoked all previous wills and named Damon Weems as the executor of the new will and given him the Power of Attorney to deal with all the financial matters of Wyatt's estate. As such, the lawyer was legally allowed to remove everything from within the bank box.

But rather than spelling out in the will who was to inherit his fortune, Wyatt had stated that that information was on the flash drive located with the will in the safe deposit box.

The problem was, the flash drive was password protected.

Kalani had returned with Damon, his dad, and his brother to the lawyer's office to open the drive.

They had spent the past half-hour trying to guess the missing password.

"We've tried all his relatives' names," Tristen said as Kalani walked back around Damon's desk and sat down in a chair between his dad and brother. "Still no luck."

"I even tried typing them in all caps, then in lower case, then in a combination of both cases," Damon added.

"Try Josh or Dillon's names," suggested Kalani. "They weren't related to Wyatt, but they were really close to him."

"Nope, *INVALID PASSWORD* again," said the lawyer after a long moment, shaking his head.

"Try their last name, Gunderson."

Again, Damon shook his head after entering the name.

"Perhaps the word is in Navajo," said Mason. "Wyatt was pretty fluent in it, I believe."

"What's the Navajo word for *turquoise*?" Kalani asked.

"I don't know," replied the lawyer.

"Let me borrow your phone, Tristen," Kalani said. "I'll Google it."

A moment later he said, "Try *Dootl'izh*." He spelled it when Damon looked up at him from his computer, puzzled.

Again, the computer screen came back *INVALID PASSWORD*.

"Try *Dineh*. Or *bilagana*," Kalani suggested.

"Nope," Damon said. "Neither one works."

Everyone in the office was silent, thinking.

"There wasn't anything in the safe deposit box that might give a hint as to what the password could be, was there?" asked Mason, breaking the silence.

Damon shook his head. "Not that I could find. You can look through all the material we found if you'd like. I removed everything from the bank vault and put all his papers in this file folder," he said, pointing to a manila folder on the corner of his desk.

Kalani got up and looked over his father's shoulder as Mason went through the papers taken from Wyatt's safe deposit box. But neither Kalani nor his dad saw anything that might be a clue to the password.

"Where was Wyatt's trading post located?" asked Kalani, sitting back down and thinking for a moment. "Maybe that's the password."

A moment later, Damon shook his head. "Nope, Sanostee didn't work either."

Again, silence in the room for a long time as everyone sat, contemplating.

Finally, Kalani broke the silence.

"Try *hozhò*," he said, spelling it for the lawyer.

Quickly, Damon Weems typed the word and waited.

The broad grin on his face told everyone that Kalani had cracked the secret of Wyatt's old clock.

Chapter 24
The Coup de Grace

Kalani stood at the back of the room, his hands jammed into his pockets to mask his nervousness. He listened to the low buzz of hushed voices, some excited, some worried. His father stood beside him leaning against the wall, his arms crossed across his chest. His body exuded calmness while Kalani struggled to hide his apprehension.

They were standing against the back wall of the conference room of the law offices of Damon Weems. Seated around a large, oval table were the friends and family of Wyatt Granger. On one side were Wyatt's neighbors Josh and Dillon, his niece Kaylee and her husband Kilian, and his muscular nephew Riley. Seated on the opposite side of the table were his other nephew, Melvin DeVille, his wife and twins, Akron and Tulsa, and a stranger Kalani didn't recognize.

"Who's the suit seated next to Mr. DeVille?" Kalani

heard Tristen ask in a soft voice. Tristen was standing on the other side of their dad.

"He's the lawyer representing Melvin in this hearing," Mason whispered back to his younger son.

"Why does he need a lawyer?" Tristen asked.

"I think he's expecting bad news and probably wants to contest any decisions made here."

"Do you think he'll have a case?" asked Kalani.

"I don't see how," his dad answered. "From what I saw of the will and the financial information on that flash drive, it looks pretty cut and dried. Melvin is out of the will."

About that time Damon Weems entered the conference room and stood at the head of the oval table. In his hand was a manila folder which he placed on the table in front of him.

"I'm glad everyone could make it today," he started. "There have been some extraordinary developments in the matter of the estate of Wyatt Granger."

He stopped, opened the folder in front of him, and took out a small stack of papers. Kalani watched as he passed out a single sheet of paper to each person seated at the table.

"This is a copy of a hand-written will, dated December 30th of last year. The original has been filed with the probate court for validation. But I expect there will be no problems certifying this will since, as you can see, it was notarized that same day. I've already spoken to the notary public who witnessed Mr. Granger's signature, and he confirms that Wyatt came to his home that morning. He also confirms that Wyatt signed the will in his presence and that the second signature and seal at the bottom are his. He also confirms he saw Wyatt fold it and placed it in his wallet."

Kalani watched everyone look at the bottom of their sheet of paper in silence. After a moment, Damon continued.

"You will also note in the first paragraph that Wyatt Granger revoked all previous wills as null and void, and that this is his last will and testament."

"What does revoke mean," Kalani heard his brother ask their dad in a soft whisper.

"It means cancelled, annulled, no longer valid," Mason whispered back. "This new will cancels the first one."

Tristen nodded his head in understanding.

"You will also note that this new will says that Wyatt Granger's estate is to be divided among the following people: his niece, Kaylee Carey and her husband Kilian; his nephew, Riley Quigley, and the brothers Josh and Dillon Gunderson. It specifically states that his nephew, Melvin DeVille, is not to inherit anything at all."

At hearing those words, Melvin exploded out of his chair, sending it crashing to the floor with a racket.

"That's preposterous!" he shouted. "We took him in and cared for him for over a year. We shared our home with him, provided a roof over his head and three-square meals a day. We drove him all around town to do his errands. We even took him to the hospital when he got sick. How dare he take us out of his will!"

Damon Weems calmly watched Melvin's outburst. When he stopped, the lawyer answered him, "I am merely informing you of what Wyatt Granger wrote in his will."

"We'll take this to court!" shouted Melvin. He was turning bright red in the face, and spit was flying from his mouth as his words spluttered out.

"Feel free to do what you feel you have to do," Damon replied calmly. "But a court battle will cost you money. Just ask your lawyer."

Melvin turned to the man sitting beside him. "You break this will and I'll pay you double."

The man looked up at Melvin standing over him. "No, my standard fees apply. In advance, I might add. I'm not sure this will can be broken."

"You're fired!" Melvin shouted at him. The lawyer calmly wiped a bit of spittle off his suit that had landed on him from Melvin's outburst. He casually stood and walked out of the room.

"This isn't over yet," Melvin shouted at Damon, turning to his wife. "Come on, Corella, kids. We're leaving."

As the DeVille family got to their feet, Akron turned to Kalani and glared at him. "You had something to do with this, didn't ya!? You just watch your back, dude!"

Kalani merely smiled at him.

ς∩

Back in the private office of Damon Weems, the lawyer looked around at the small group of friends and family mentioned in Wyatt Granger's will. Also present were Kalani, his brother Tristen, and their dad. Everyone was seated in front of Damon's big desk as the lawyer casually leaned on the front of it, facing the group.

"How in the world did you find the new will?" Dillon asked the lawyer.

"I'm afraid you'll have to ask Kalani Henderson that question," he replied. "I had very little to do with it. He did all the detective work and tracked down all the clues. He presented me with a *fait accompli*, an accomplished feat, all tied up with a pretty bow." He smiled at Kalani, seated at the end of the semi-circle of chairs as all eyes turned to him.

Slowly and carefully Kalani began his tale. As he mentioned what he learned from each of the people seated in the room, they nodded their heads in agreement. When he got to the problem of opening the files on the flash drive, Damon reached back behind him and picked up a stack of papers off his desk.

When Kalani had finished, he handed each person a sheet of paper. Kalani stared at his copy in shock. It was a break-down of Wyatt's estate and what each person was to inherit. Kalani had not seen the figures before. Since Damon had been named executor of the will, he had elected to keep secret the information on the flash drive once it was unlocked.

Kalani sucked in his breath when he saw the vast estate of Wyatt Granger. Wyatt had several million dollars in various banks around the area. He also had a large portfolio of stock market investments. According to the sheet in his hand, the portfolio itself was worth another million dollars or so. Finally, Wyatt owned the huge property next to the Gunderson brothers.

The group was silent as they looked in shock disbelief at the huge fortune Wyatt had accumulated. There was enough so that each of his heirs would be a millionaire. Kalani heard Kaylee start to sob quietly as she read her inheritance.

In the will, Wyatt divided the money in the numerous bank accounts equally among Kaylee and Kilian, Riley, Josh and Dillon. He also stipulated that the yearly dividend income from the stocks and bonds would go his niece and nephew so that they would never have to worry again about a steady income.

He gave the property next to the Gunderson brothers to Josh and Dillon so they would have a place to open their own mechanics shop. Their portion of the money deposited in the banks would ensure that both brothers could attend any mechanics school they wanted. They would also be able to furnish a new shop with the latest tools and equipment.

To his lawyer and friend, Damon Weems, Wyatt left the responsibility of managing the stock portfolio, stipulating that he could pay himself ten per cent of whatever the stocks earned each year, thus giving his friend motivation to insure a large, steady income from high paying dividends for the lawyer, Kaylee, and Riley.

Kalani looked up from his sheet and saw a mixture of amazement and joy on everyone's face. He saw the Gunderson brothers exchange a silent look.

"None of this would have been possible without your help, Kalani," Josh said softly. "We owe you a big reward."

Kilian, Kaylee, and Riley all nodded their heads in agreement.

"I think we should buy him a car, any one of his choosing," said Dillon. "What kind would you like?"

"I don't want anything from you guys," Kalani said hurriedly. "Seeing you get paid back for your kindness to Wyatt is reward enough for me."

"Besides, he doesn't have his driver's license yet," his brother added.

"Yeah, I've got to get a ton more hours driving with an adult before I can go down to take my driving test," he said.

"No, I think you've met your fifty-hour requirement," said his father.

Kalani looked at his dad. "No, I haven't. I've been keeping track, and I'm not even halfway there yet. And I have to wait six months before I can test."

Mason smiled at his son. "No, you've met the hourly requirement."

Kalani looked puzzled at this. He knew he wasn't anywhere near the required fifty hours driving with an adult. He also knew his dad was a stickler for following the rules.

"Remember, I'm the one that signs off on your having met the requirements. And after talking with Deputy Raybon at the sheriff's department in Colorado, who told me how you drove him and the bandit to the hospital, I think I'll fudge the rest of the hours. We'll schedule you for a driving test as soon as your six-month probation is up."

Kalani's face lit up.

"Besides, I'm tired of you badgering me about taking the pickup on errands."

Chapter 25
Kalani's Reward

A few weeks later, Kalani was updating his list of contacts into his new cell phone when he got a text. His parents had decided he deserved some kind of reward for successfully finding Wyatt Granger's lost will. They were proud of him for his determination and stick-to-it'ness, so they bought him the latest cell phone on the market.

The text was from Dillon Gunderson who asked him to drop by.

"Can I borrow the pickup to run over to Josh and Dillon's?" Kalani asked his dad who was cleaning the barbeque grill on the back patio.

"Sure," he answered. "Just be back in time for supper. I'm grilling hamburgers."

"Can I invite Josh and Dillon?"

"Sure. I haven't seen them since the reading of the will."

Several minutes later, Kalani pulled up to the

Gunderson brothers' home and sat there, amazed at the changes he saw. The house had been repainted and a new roof put on. New windows had been installed, the kind that kept the house cool in the summer and warm in the winter.

The barn where he and Tristen had taken refuge from the storm so long ago was also in the process of being repaired. There was now electricity to it since the interior was lit by bright, florescent lights. The missing boards on the exterior had been replaced, and there was scaffolding set up so the roof could be re-shingled. Cans of paint and several rollers told Kalani that a new paint job was in the offing. When he climbed out of the pickup, Kalani saw Josh and Dillon walk toward him from the barn, cleaning their hands on new, red garage rags.

"We're not equipped to handle pickups yet," he heard Dillon joke. When Kalani held out his hand to shake Dillon's, he was surprised by the big hug he got instead.

"We just wanted to thank you again for what you did for us," he heard Dillon say. "We'd still like to give you something as a reward."

"I really don't want you to spend any of your inheritance on me," Kalani replied. "You two deserve everything you got from Wyatt."

"Are you sure there's nothing we can do for you?"

"Sure, there is. You can come over and have hamburgers with us again."

"It's a deal!" Josh replied. "We'll be over after we clean up."

∽

Later that evening, the Henderson family sat around the backyard patio after a meal of hamburgers cooked on the outdoor grill. Everyone was full and content except Kalani. He looked sadly at the empty platter where the patties had been kept warm on the grill.

There was still a pair of buns and some barbequed beans left. He put the buns, open-faced, on his plate then covered them in beans like a Sloppy Joe. He parents just shook their heads in amazement at his appetite.

"Kalani tells me you're fixing up your house and barn," said Mason to the Gunderson brothers.

"Yes sir, we've got the house all painted, a new roof put on, and better windows installed," said Josh. "The barn is almost done too. We can actually do repairs in it now without having to worry about the roof leaking when it rains."

"And Josh starts classes soon at San Juan College in their small engine repair department," Dillon added.

"Be sure to take some business and accounting classes while you're at it," Mason said. "You'll need them for that new business you're opening up."

"I plan to," said Josh. "Mr. Weems talked to us about that very thing when we were discussing how to set up our repair shop. He's going to help us keep the financial books until I learn some accounting."

"What do you plan to do with Wyatt's old house next door to you?" asked Tammy Henderson.

"We haven't quite decided," said Josh. "We may fix it up and rent it out, perhaps as a low-income house, to help other people struggling with their finances."

"Or convert it into a really big shop to do repairs in," added Dillon. "It just depends on how big our business grows."

"Have you heard the latest on the DeVilles?" asked Dillon in the pause that followed.

"No, what happened?" asked Kalani. "Did they go to jail for old-folks abuse?"

"Almost as bad," laughed Josh. "Melvin may go to jail if the District Attorney in Colorado can prove he gave the key to their cabin to the gang of thieves who burglarized it. There was no sign of a forced entry as you remember. He was planning to collect the insurance from the robbery."

"Melvin had to declare bankruptcy as well," added Dillon. "Seems the whole family ran up a lot of bills between the time Wyatt died and when you found the second will. Akron even wrecked a brand-new Corvette. Totaled it with no insurance."

"Yeah, I remember Mr. DeVille bragging they would soon have a ton of money. He said that when we dropped by to sell those tickets to the Navajo Taco dinner. Right before that crazy trip to Vallecito. Guess they were counting their chickens before they hatched."

"How did you find out about all this?" asked Mason.

"Mr. Weems told us at one of our meetings with him," said Dillon. "Seems he gets all the inside scoop from his lawyer friends."

Kalani just smiled.

∽

"Are you sure there's nothing we can get you as a reward?" Josh asked Kalani. "You went to a lot of trouble to help us. We feel we should give you something in return, something to show you how much we appreciate you."

"As I said before, I'm just happy to help you two out for being so kind to Wyatt," Kalani replied.

"Well, we intend to ask you that question every time we see you," said Dillon. "So, you'd better think of something we can give you."

Kalani sat for a moment before looking up at

the two brothers. "If you really insist, maybe there is something you could give me."

Both of the Gundersons looked at him.

"What about that old clock of Wyatt Granger's as a souvenir of my first mystery."

Josh and Dillon looked at each other. "It's a deal!" they said together.

Kalani sat back in his chair, a sad look on his face. After the excitement of cracking the secret of the missing will, how was he going to spend the rest of his summer? Everything else would be a let-down. Not even video games at the mall or Rez ball with Danner could match the excitement of solving a mystery.

About the Author

Photo by Rick Greenacre

Jack Yerby is a retired high school French and English teacher living in the Four Corners area of New Mexico.

He enjoys a good story, especially one with a bit of a mystery to it. And by writing young adult mysteries, he hopes to pass along his love of reading to the next generation, especially the boys.

When not in the gym, Jack enjoys traveling to different countries, and in particular, France. He lives with his cats, Midnight and Twilight, who take turns napping in his lap while he writes on the computer.

You can find more about Jack and his writing at http://www.jackyerbyauthor.com.

Also by Jack Yerby

The Secret of the Haunted House

There's a mysterious light in the old, burned down house across the road. Could it be the ghost of old lady Hampton? Or maybe the firefighter who died trying to save her? And why is Mrs. Tsosie so afraid to get close to the property?

Kennny doesn't believe in ghosts, but when strange footprints are discovered in the neighborhood, he and his brother search the old ruins for clues. Kenny knows he is getting close to unraveling the mystery when he discovers firsthand just how dangerous crime solving can be!

The Secret of the Haunted House
Chapter 1

"It is too haunted!" said eleven-year-old James, his pudgy hands firmly on his hips.

"No, it's not!" said his brother Kenny, putting his hands on his slim hips. Kenny was three years older and several inches taller. And that made him always right. Or so he thought.

"Yes, it is!" said James. He stuck his chubby chin out in a determined manner.

"No it's not!" said Kenny, throwing his chin out. He dared his brother to say anything more.

"Is!"

"Not!"

"Is!"

"Not!"

The faces of the two boys were only inches apart, and the fight looked like it was going to get physical.

At that point Mike, their seventeen-year-old brother, stepped up to his two younger siblings, put his hands behind their heads and banged their foreheads together. They both looked up at him, surprised.

"How do you know it's haunted?" Mike asked James. He looked down at his little brother from his six-foot-three height.

"Cause Katie said it was," James said, rubbing his forehead where a red spot was forming. Kenny was doing the same thing to a similar red spot on his own head.

"And you believe Katie?" Mike said. He crossed his hands on his chest and looked down at James in amazement. Katie was sixteen and often pulled pranks on her two younger brothers.

"Remember how she told you that you could catch a bird by putting salt on its tail?"

James looked sheepishly at his feet. Even though Katie's prank happened years ago when he was a lot younger, no one in the family let him forget it.

"You spent all day chasing birds with a saltshaker," Mike continued. "It never occurred to you that if you were close enough to put salt on its tail, you could reach out and just grab it."

"Well, how do you explain that light across the dirt road in the Hampton house last night?" James said looking up at Mike.

"What light?" said Kenny, interrupting his brother. "I didn't see a light over there."

"That's because you were too busy playing that silly ol' video game to come see. I called you but you never even looked up from your computer."

"I did too come see," Kenny said, "but there wasn't anything there. You're just a kid. You believe everything people tell you."

"I do not!" said James.

"You do too!" Kenny retorted.

"Do not!"

"Do too!"

At this point Mike turned away, threw up his hands in frustration, and walked away. "I give up," he said to himself. "They just like to argue."

Later that night in the bedroom they shared, Kenny heard his younger brother ask from the top bunk, "Hey Kenny, do you believe in ghosts?"

"Naw," he said from the bottom bunk. "They're just stories for little kids. I'm too grown up to believe in them anymore."

"But what about Katie?" James asked. "She says they're real."

"You know she likes to tell you crazy stuff and make you believe it," Kenny said. "Just like when she told you the Boogie…"

He stopped in mid-sentence, remembering that even at eleven years old, James was still afraid of monsters in the dark. When Katie had told him the Boogie Man lived under the bottom bunk, James had insisted on having the top bunk. To this day he never slept with one foot over the edge of the bed for fear the monster would grab it and drag him down to its lair.

"Just look at Mike. And Mom," Kenny said, continuing in a hurry. He hoped James didn't notice his slip of the tongue. "They don't say there are ghosts."

"Yeah," said James from the top bunk, "but they don't say there aren't any ghosts. Just because they don't say something exists doesn't mean they're not real."

Kenny couldn't think of an answer to that. After a pause, he asked, "Did you really see a light over there last night?" His voice was quiet and thoughtful.

He knew James didn't tell lies just to get attention. His little brother always told the truth, even if it got him in trouble.

"Yeah, I did!" James said excitedly. He leaned over the edge of the top bunk to look at Kenny. "I tried to get you to come see, but you took so long on the computer you missed it."

"What did it look like, that light?" Kenny asked, his hands behind his head as he looked up at his little brother. "Was it like the ghost's whole body was shining? Or was the light little, like a flashlight or something?"

"I don't know," James said, "I just saw light shining

through the cracks in the walls and in the gaps where the windows used to be."

"I'll bet it's the ghost of that fireman who died in the fire," said Katie, poking her head into the room. Kenny jumped at her sudden appearance.

"You mean the one who was trying to save ol' lady Hampton?" James said. He craned his head up to look at his sister while still leaning over the edge of the top bunk.

"Yeah," Katie answered. "He was in the house looking for her when the roof fell in on him and burned him up. They never found his body."

"That doesn't mean he's a ghost," said Kenny. "If they never found his body, then he probably didn't die." He sat up in the bottom bunk and pulled the sheets up to his chin. He was self-conscious of his skinny body.

"Oh yeah it does," said Katie as she walked into the room. "He's still in the house trying to rescue her. And sometimes when there's a storm, you can hear him calling, 'Where are you, lady?'"

"That's just the wind!" said Kenny. "I thought I heard voices coming from over there too, but it was just the wind making it sound like somebody calling out."

After a moment of silence, James continued from the top bunk, "I wonder why they never found her body." He was still leaning over the edge, and Kenny saw him straining his neck to look at their sister.

"They did, silly," said Katie. "She was in bed, all burned up by the fire."

"She slept through the fire?" said James, puzzled. "Wouldn't the sirens have waked her up?"

"Not if she wanted to die," said Katie. "She committed suicide by setting the house on fire."

"Why would she do that?"

"She didn't want to live anymore because her son robbed a bank and was a criminal," said Katie. "It made her sorry she ever had a kid. She set fire to her house after he was killed in that shoot-out with the cops."

"Wouldn't getting burned up in the house turn her into a ghost?" said Kenny. "People who commit suicide have to stay on earth and haunt the place where they died."

"How do you know that?" said Katie slyly. "I thought you didn't believe in ghosts."

"I saw it on the internet," Kenny said with a yawn. "Now, turn out the light and leave so I can get to sleep." And he snuggled down in his bed, the sheets still pulled up to his chin.